
★

I COULD ALMOST HEAR
THE WHEELS TURNING.

He hadn't believed in a mugger from the start. Now Sharon had presented him with a link between two possible violences. Ted Valentine, beaten to death, stripped of all identification, hopefully to become a nameless corpse in the morgue; thirty-one months ago Vic Lewis had vanished, possibly the victim of another violence. Beware young lovers with a yen for an older glamor girl—who just happens to be going on the *Dick Thomas Show*. Not very sensible, but I was sure that's what Chambrun was thinking.

★

HUGH PENTECOST

BEWARE YOUNG LOVERS

WORLDWIDE®

TORONTO • NEW YORK • LONDON • PARIS
AMSTERDAM • STOCKHOLM • HAMBURG
ATHENS • MILAN • TOKYO • SYDNEY

BEWARE YOUNG LOVERS

A Worldwide Mystery/October 1990

First published by Dodd, Mead & Company, Inc.

ISBN 0-373-26057-1

PART ONE

ONE

I KNEW from past experience that the next five days were going to be hell-on-wheels for me. I didn't need any trouble on this last night before the big headache began and I resented it when it came.

"Why me?" I demanded of Mr. Cardoza when he called my apartment and told me I was needed.

"Because the boss, who could handle this perfectly, has chosen to take a powder. You, Mr. Haskell, are the number two trouble-shooter in this glamor palace," Cardoza said in his smooth, slightly accented way. Never any panic or anxiety from Cardoza, even if the roof was falling in on his segment of our world.

Our world is the Beaumont, New York's top luxury hotel, perhaps the world's top luxury hotel. Mr. Cardoza is the maitre d' in the Blue Lagoon, our night-club. I am Mark Haskell, with the title of Public Relations Director. The boss is Pierre Chambrun, the legendary manager of the Beaumont; he is the king, the boss, the mayor of what is like a small city, the iron fist in the velvet glove. He is rarely unavailable, rarely "takes a powder." There is a rule by which all of us who work for Chambrun operate. You may not make a mistake. If you have any doubts about how to handle a sticky situation, you contact The Man. Chambrun is The Man. He will decide what to do, and if what he decides is a mistake he will take the blame. If anyone else makes a wrong decision, having decided not to consult The Man, he is likely to find himself among the unemployed.

Cardoza's problem that Sunday evening, before the beginning of the week I knew was going to be hellish, was that a lady, alone at a table in the elegant Blue Lagoon, had gone berserk, was shouting insults at the other customers, smashing china and glassware. Cardoza's answer to that would seem to be simple. Call Jerry Dodd, the hotel's security officer, and have the lady forcibly ejected.

Only she wasn't just any lady. She was Sharon Brand.

Any reader who had gone to the movies in the last thirty years knows that Sharon Brand has been Hollywood's top glamor queen, following in the footsteps of Garbo, Lombard, Shearer, Crawford, Russell. She is a three-time Oscar winner; a Tony winner for a brilliant Broadway performance a few years back. She is a fine actress and still a great beauty at fifty. She must, I thought, be at least fifty, whatever her press agent may say. Just going back over her career makes it impossible to guess younger.

There was one other thing that made handling a berserk Sharon Brand a touchy business. She was a long-time customer of the Beaumont's. The hotel was her home-away-from-home when she came to New York. When she did a Broadway play, she stayed with us for the run. If that wasn't enough, she was more than a paying guest to Pierre Chambrun. He admired her, they were friends. When she stayed with us, she frequently spent time with The Man in his penthouse apartment. Not a love affair, I think, but just a sort of mutual admiration society.

Handling a berserk Sharon Brand called for Chambrun's expertise and personal friendship with the lady. He wasn't available and so I was elected, God help me.

The Blue Lagoon is a favorite after-theater hangout for the rich. You have to be rich to enjoy anything the Beaumont has to offer. I had been in my second-floor apartment when Cardoza called, so it was only a matter of minutes when I joined him inside the red velvet rope that shut off the curious and the hopeful without reservations from the paying guests, seated around the dimly lit, blue-oriented room. On the bandstand, at the far end of the room, Willie Connors was at the baby grand piano making magic out of old ragtime. He plays between the featured acts that should have been in progress now—a little after midnight. Sharon Brand's blowout had evidently delayed the regular schedule.

Cardoza, looking like an elegant Spanish grandee, was waiting for me.

"You wouldn't believe," he said.

I looked out into the room. It was crowded except for three or four tables in the center that surrounded a small table at which Sharon Brand sat. Her hair is golden blond, probably not real any more. With her lovely bone structure, wide mouth, bright blue eyes, she was more like Carol Lombard than any of her other predecessors in movie fame. Around the table were scattered pieces of broken china, broken glasses, the remains of food that had been served her. Every eye in the place was focused on her. A white-faced waiter approached her, very tentative, carrying a drink on a tray. He put it down on her table and beat a hasty retreat. She took a sip of it, and then smashed the glass, drink and all, on the floor.

"I told you dry, you sonofabitch!" she shouted at the waiter. "Try again!"

"Bombed out," I said to Cardoza.

"I don't think she's had much to drink," he said, surprising me. "She's ordered about ten martinis, but she hasn't had more than sip from each before she's tossed it away. I—uh—tried to talk to her. No dice. 'I don't socialize with waiters,' she told me." He gestured toward the room. "An unknown person creates this kind of disturbance and this room would be empty," he said. "People demanding refunds, God knows what else. But she's Sharon Brand. It's as if they were all watching, fascinated, a great performance by a great actress."

"And aren't they?" I said. "You tried everywhere to locate The Man?"

"He told the switchboard he was leaving the hotel for a couple of hours. Didn't say where he was going."

I took a deep breath. "Well, here goes nothing," I said.

I could hear the undertone of subdued but excited voices as I went down the three steps into the room and headed for Sharon Brand's table. I felt as if I was walking into a spotlight on center stage to play a scene for which I didn't have a script. Afterwards I realized that an electrician backstage actually had focused a baby-blue pin spot on the lady.

The first thing I noticed as I came close to her, stood just beside her, was that she smelled absolutely wonderful. The perfume she was wearing was probably unique, made for her alone, seductive, pulse-raising. Then she looked up at me and those bright blue eyes bored holes in me. I suspected she could read the label on the inside of my shirt collar. The eyes were bright, they were also hostile, and at the same time I had the feeling I was looking into two deep, tragic wells.

"What are you, some kind of a house dick?" she asked me. Her voice was deep, husky, a voice that had excited American males for thirty years.

I sat down in the empty chair next to hers. I thought she looked around for something to throw at me, but she'd thrown everything within reach.

"We have met before," I said, "but there's no reason you should remember. I'm Mark Haskell."

"I remember," she said. "You're Pierre's errand boy. Where is he? I expected him before this."

"That why you've been making a scene? To attract him?"

"No. But I thought it would attract him. Thrown to the office boy, am I?"

"He's out of the hotel. He doesn't know what's going on. If he did, he'd be here. He's very fond of you."

Her blue-shaded eyelids fluttered and closed for a moment. Then she looked straight at me again. "How old are you? About thirty-five?"

"About," I said.

"Neither the one thing nor the other," she said.

"I don't follow," I said.

"You're not old enough or young enough," she said.

I grinned at her. "I like to think I'm maturing," I said. "You know, the show has to go on here, Miss Brand, and it can't while you're holding center stage. We don't have any entertainers who can match you."

To my astonishment her eyes brimmed with tears. "Do you think you could take me out of here, acting like an escort and not a cop?" she asked.

I leaned close to her and kissed her cheek. I thought she might slug me, but she didn't. I stood up and held out both my hands to her. She took them and let me pull her up to her feet.

"I was stood up," she whispered. "They all know it. If they think it was you, and you just came late—"

I linked her arm in mine and bent down, as though I was whispering to her. We walked toward the velvet rope like that. Suddenly, behind us, somebody started to applaud. It grew in volume. On the stage Willie Connors began to play softly. "It Was Just One of Those Things."

Cardoza unhooked the velvet rope. "Good night, Miss Brand," he said.

She began to laugh as I walked her out into the lobby. There was a note of hysteria in it.

"Easy does it," I said. "Where would you like me to take you?"

"My suite," she said. "Fourteen B."

We headed for the bank of elevators. I don't know if she was aware of how closely we were watched. Jerry Dodd, our head of Security, was watching, and Mike Maggio, the night bell captain, and Fred Iverson, the man on the front desk. I guess they'd been ready to move in if I'd failed.

I took her to Chambrun's private elevator and pressed the button for Fourteen. It's self-service. The car started up noiselessly.

"Anyone who would stand you up," I said to that beautiful woman, still holding her arm, "is either out of his mind or was run over by a taxi on his way here."

She gave me a bitter smile. "He's just a young punk laughing himself sick somewhere at an old bag," she said.

I AM NEITHER a psychiatrist nor a psychologist, but being in the hotel business at the level of the Beaumont, you come to be, like it or not, a student of human behavior, human foibles, eccentricities, neuroses, psychoses. You could say the Beaumont is like a walled city with its own restaurants, bars, shops; its bank, hospital, travel service, police force, and government, centered in Chambrun's second floor office. Everything that happens in every other city happens inside the confines of the Beaumont. People get born there, married there, and die there; there are murders and suicides; there are thieves and con men always circulating; wives betray their husbands and husbands betray their wives; old men die from overworked hearts in the beds of young women they scarcely know; big business meets in the private rooms to plan the next rip-off of the ordinary citizens; high-class hookers are temptingly visible in the bars and restaurants.

There is one thing different about the Beaumont from the average city. Aside from half of dozen people who own cooperative units on the top floors, the population is transient, always moving, always changing. The swarms of people who come and go round the clock have no roots in the hotel. It is a luxurious way station for people who have business in the world's greatest city. They have no sense of community about the place where they stay temporarily. Hotel security is not like the cop on the beat who knows the people in his area and what to expect from them. We are a little bit like the defensive players on a football team, always trying to guess in advance what play the opposing quarterback will call in the huddle. We have to be ready for anything and everything—including what makes a famous and beautiful lady go haywire in a public place, and how to handle her without damage to the hotel or to herself.

We walked down the corridor on Fourteen toward Suite B. Sharon Brand's arm was still linked in mine, and her long, slim fingers, cold as icicles, were fastened on my wrist. The lady, I thought, is afraid of something, hanging onto me for dear life.

I tried to remember what I knew about her, beyond the usual gossip column jazz. You see, the guests at the Beaumont might not be pleased to know how complete a dossier we have on some of them. Every morning at precisely nine thirty I meet with Chambrun in his office on the second floor, joined by Betsy Ruysdale, his fabulous secretary. He has finished his breakfast, served by Jacques Fresney, the head chef. It is an elaborate meal; chafing dishes in which Fresney can prepare omelettes, a microwave oven in which he can broil a breakfast steak, or some kind of fish or bacon or ham; hot dishes of chicken hash or kidney stew. The Man doesn't eat again until nine at night, when he is served a gourmet dinner in his penthouse. At nine-thirty in the morning I find him sitting at his carved Florentine desk in an office that looks more like a gracious living room than a place of business. Short, stocky, black-haired, Chambrun has bright black eyes buried in deep pouches that can mirror compassion, humor, or take on the baleful look of a hanging judge if he is angry. Always in front of him on his desk at nine-thirty are a cup of Turkish coffee, prepared by Miss Ruysdale, a box of his flat, Egyptian cigarettes, and the registration cards from the day before. New guests. When a new guest registers, several people make notations on a card before Chambrun sees it. Credit ratings are supplied by Mr. Atterbury, the credit manager, ranging from "Unlimited" down through A, B, and C. The cost of a stay at the Beaumont is no laughing matter. Security supplies other information. A is for an alcoholic. WC for a woman chaser; XX for a man double-crossing his wife; WXX for a woman double-crossing her husband; G for gay. If the guest is a repeater, you may see Chambrun's initials, P.C., on the bottom of the card. That means The Man knows something about the guest that isn't for public consumption.

I remembered, two days ago, Sharon Brand's card being on Chambrun's desk. Her credit was unlimited. Why not? She must have made millions in films. There was no other information on the card except Chambrun's initials. If there was anything special to know about Sharon Brand, it was locked away in Chambrun's private store of information.

He had passed her card to me two mornings ago. "A very great lady in her particular world," he said. "She is used to red-carpet treatment and she has earned it. We make sure she doesn't miss it here, Mark."

The lady and I had reached the door of Fourteen B. She handed me the little gold evening bag she was carrying in her free hand.

"My key," she said. "Would you mind?"

I fished her key out of the bag and opened the door for her.

"Please come in," she said.

Fourteen B is one of the more luxurious suites. There is a living room, a small dining alcove and kitchenette, two bedrooms and two baths. None of the suites in the Beaumont are furnished alike. Fourteen B is elegant early American, with a genuine Grant Wood painting on one wall worth a small fortune. There are bookshelves containing a carefully chosen library of American authors. It looks lived in, even though the new tenant has only just arrived. You could simply be taking over a friend's apartment.

Lights were on in the suite. It was standard practice for the night maid, when she came in to turn down beds, to leave rooms lighted. A guest, in an unfamiliar place, might find himself disturbed by fumbling for light switches.

Sharon Brand and I walked through the little vestibule and into the living room. I had the feeling that the tips of her long fingernails were drawing blood on my wrist.

"Would you very much mind looking in the other rooms?" she asked in her husky voice.

"Looking for what?" I asked.

"Just to be sure," she said. She sounded almost like a little girl, frightened of imaginary villains. But I supposed, perhaps, it was a part of her life. There is no kind of secure privacy for anyone as famous and publicly glamorous as Sharon Brand. Some creep could be hiding somewhere, waiting to demand her autograph. Or worse, some peeping Tom hidden to take a look at a famous body when she undressed for bed—perhaps even planning an assault on her. Nothing like that could happen in the Beaumont, I told myself, but she couldn't be sure of that and there was no reason not to reassure her.

I disengaged her fingers from my wrist. There were two little gouges there.

"Mine is the room on the left," she said.

I walked down the short corridor past the kitchenette and opened the door to the left. A lamp was burning on the table beside the big four-poster bed. The bed was turned down. There was a white, lace-frilled negligee laid out, silver slippers on the rug just below it. The room smelled deliciously of woman—of very special woman. I glanced over at the dressing table. On it was the equipment for a small beauty salon: bottles, jars, powder boxes, perfume sprays, a full makeup kit, silver-backed hair brush and hand mirror. Being beautiful in public was the lady's business.

I laughed at myself as I looked under the bed. I opened the sliding closet doors and was confronted by endless dresses and gowns, a couple of dozen pairs of shoes, boots, pumps, and slippers on the racks behind the doors. I parted some of the dresses, still laughing at myself, and looked to see if anyone could be hiding there. There was no one, of course. I checked the bathroom. No one and nothing.

I went back out into the hall. She was standing at the living room end, waiting, I guessed, for a report.

"All clear," I told her.

She gestured toward the door across the hall from hers. I opened it to darkness. There was no light left there by the maid, presumably because it wasn't occupied. I reached for the main switch to the right of the door.

The bed was not turned down.

"No one," I called out to Sharon Brand.

"The closet!" she called back.

The closet was empty and I so reported.

"The bureau drawers?" There was a kind of urgency in her voice.

There was nothing in the bureau or on it. I told her that as I checked the deserted bathroom.

Then I heard a cry from her, a piercing wail of frustration, anger, perhaps I should use the word "agony.'' It took me out of there and back to the living room on the run.

She was sitting on the couch, doubled over, pounding at the pillows with her fist. She let out that frightened cry again and looked up at me. Her blue eyes were brimming with tears.

''That bastard!'' she said to me, her voice now hoarse and low. ''That miserable bastard!''

At that moment the front door buzzer sounded. She sat straight up, staring toward the vestibule.

''You don't want to see anyone just now,'' I said.

''See who it is!'' she said.

I went to the vestibule, closing the living-room door behind me. No one should get to see her the way she looked at the moment. I opened the outside door and a great, cool wave of relief passed over me. Chambrun stood there.

''How are things?'' he asked.

''Pretty bad,'' I said, ''although I haven't had time to find out why.''

The door behind us opened and Sharon Brand was there.

''Pierre!'' she cried out. ''Oh my God, Pierre!''

She ran to him, threw her arms around him, sobbing uncontrollably. He held her gently, stroking her golden hair.

''That miserable bastard has walked out on me, Pierre!'' Sharon managed to tell him.

Chambrun turned his head, still soothing her, to look at me. ''Thanks for taking care of things, Mark,'' he said.

That was worth a day's pay.

''You've got a tough day tomorrow,'' Chambrun said. ''I'll take over from here.''

TWO

I HAVE MENTIONED earlier that I was looking forward to five days of a particular kind of hell. They would begin tomorrow—today, as a matter of fact. My watch told me that it was one-thirty in the morning as I reached my quarters on the second floor, down the hall from Chambrun's office. I needed to grab whatever shuteye I could before, like Henny-Penny, the sky fell in on me.

I will never know why Chambrun had been persuaded to let the Dick Thomas Show take over the Beaumont's main ballroom for a week once every year. Tomorrow—or today—would begin the fifth time around. Our regular routines would be thrown out of kilter, the hotel would be overrun by swarms of goons who would never come into the place at any other time. We would be confronted by dictatorial demands from Dick Thomas's staff, his sponsors. Our regular guests, who expected peace and quiet and elegance, would be jostled and shouted at. The lobby, the ballroom, the main-level bars and restaurants would be littered with candy wrappers, empty cigarette packages, beer cans, pop bottles. The regular customers would be shouting complaints, and the Dick Thomas camp followers would be shouting complaints. It was my job, a hopeless one, to keep some kind of sanity intact.

The Dick Thomas Show is an American phenomenon, not unique. Anyone who watches television with any regularity has seen its counterparts—the Mike

Douglas Show, the Merv Griffin Show, the Dinah Shore Show. They all follow the same formula for ninety minutes a day. Mike Douglas, and Merv Griffin, and Dinah Shore are all better-than-average singers of popular ballads. Their special gifts are a talent for interviewing people. Some doll has written a book which might be called *My Love Affair with Frank Sinatra*, a kiss-and-tell piece of garbage. Mike, and Merv, and Dinah, and Dick Thomas interview her, thus promoting the sale of the book. A country-and-western singer performs a number from his—or her—new album, thus promoting the sale of records. A movie star modestly discusses the tragedies of being famous, thus promoting his—or her—new film. A pseudo-doctor talks gravely about child abuse in America, thus promoting his fascinating new article in *Playboy* magazine. A young starlet is properly shy about discussing a nude scene in her latest film. And on and on. Ninety minutes a day!

The live audience, fifteen hundred of them each day in our ballroom, gets titillated for free. They see and hear Dick Thomas, who could pass for a relative of Robert Redford; they see and hear the stars, the singers, and the gossip purveyors, the dope addict who got cured of the habit through yoga. On the Thomas show there is a fabulous eight-piece orchestra with Jake Floyd at the piano. Jake is bald, probably sixty, and even on the air always has the stub of an unlighted cigar in the corner of his mouth. He can, on request, play any jazz or show tune ever written. He once told me he started out playing piano in a house of ill repute in New Orleans where the management put up a hundred dollars for any guest who could ask Jake for a tune he couldn't play.

"I couldn't afford to lose," Jake told me once, "because the management didn't have a hundred bucks!"

Jake and his boys can pick up anything the situation calls for, accompany the singers, comment with musical stings on the jokes and jibes. For me, Jake almost makes the show worth the watching.

In addition to Jake's band there is a camera crew of half a dozen men, a lighting expert, a set designer who dresses the stage for each show, plus an army of public relations people, advertising salesmen, talent procurers, and God knows who else. All Dick Thomas has to do on the show is sing his opening ballad and interview his guests. He was particularly expert at the interviewing part of it because of a woman named Laura Sayles, who reads all the books, researches all the performers, and briefs Dick Thomas on precisely what questions to ask. Audiences think Dick is a genius who does an incredible amount of homework. Laura Sayles, a Twiggy-thin doll whose face is almost obscured by enormous, round, shell-rimmed glasses, is the real genius. Dick Thomas seems totally unaware of what everyone else close to his show knows. Plain, hardworking, often brilliant, Laura Sayles was desperately in love with Dick Thomas. She might as well have a sign painted on her flat chest, but Dick Thomas can't see it or read it—or doesn't want to bother. But he depends on her for the lifeblood of his show.

It was this strange menagerie that I was going to have to face up to in a few hours. They rehearsed from ten till two, the show goes on the air, live, at four till five thirty. You may not see it at that time of day, because it's syndicated to individual stations all over the country, played at different times that fit their schedules.

But what went on in our ballroom at five was live, done before a live audience. That wild-eyed audience would be milling around the Beaumont from breakfast on, waiting for their chance to get into the ballroom. There would be a thousand or more who wouldn't make it, and they'd rush to the bars in the hotel and in the neighborhood to catch on television what they were missing.

It was uncharacteristic of Chambrun to let it happen at all. Swiss-watch routines in the hotel were the name of his game. Why he would let them cave in for a week every year was beyond me. The hotel, of course, got massive public exposure on TV sets around the country for a week, but free advertising wasn't a good enough explanation for me. We didn't need advertising. We couldn't begin to take care of the people who wanted to stay with us as it was. I asked Chambrun about it after the first wild week five years ago. Why open up our facilities to Dick Thomas? He seemed angered by the question.

"If you don't know the answer to that, Mark, you're not as bright as I thought you were," he said.

After five years I still don't know the answer.

THE SWITCHBOARD CALLS me every morning at eight-thirty. That gives me an hour to shave, shower, dress, and make myself some coffee and toast in my kitchenette before I meet Chambrun in his office at exactly nine-thirty.

It was like any day. Chambrun had finished his breakfast and was sitting at his desk. Jacques Fresney, the chef, without asking served me a cup of American coffee. Betsy Ruysdale, The Man's secretary, had already served him his first cup of Turkish coffee and he was shuffling through the registration cards, not more than half a dozen that morning.

"Nothing very exciting here, Ruysdale," Chambrun said, and handed Betsy the cards.

He neuters her by calling her Ruysdale, but there is nothing neuter about that lady. I suppose she would admit to being thirty-five. She is tall, with reddish hair and a figure that would have the cowboys whistling at her. I don't think Chambrun could get along without her, and I'm not referring to the rumor that there may be more between them than the boss-secretary relationship. She has the knack of anticipating his needs, of being half a step ahead of him whenever he needs or wants something. If she wasn't clearly off limits, I'd have been after her under a full head of steam.

"I imagine the lobby is crawling with Dick Thomas fans," I said. "I'd better be off." I grinned at Chambrun. "See you in five days if I survive."

There was a twinkle of humor in his dark eyes. "I count on your making it," he said. "But before you go into battle, I'd like to talk to you both about last night. You, particularly, are entitled, Mark."

"You're talking about Sharon Brand?" I asked.

"What else happened last night?" He was concerned about Sharon, I realized.

"It was apparently quite a scene she played in the Blue Lagoon," Ruysdale said. She gave me a wry little smile. "Cardoza called me for help, but I suggested Mark was a better bet. He is, after all, a man."

Chambrun's eyes narrowed as he lit one of his Egyptian cigarettes with his gold lighter. "Right decision," he said. "She feels women are her enemies."

"Why not?" Ruysdale asked, with just a touch of acid. "She's been after other women's men forever."

She gave Chambrun a steady, almost questioning look. After him, she was asking. He ignored the question.

"The last five years have been a different story for her," he said. "Before that you're right of course. She had, or is rumored to have had, affairs with every male star in Hollywood. You two know her history?"

"One marriage," Ruysdale said. "More lovers than Cleopatra."

"Thirty-two years ago she married a young actor named Carleton Delaney," Chambrun said. "She was eighteen, he was ten years older. They were both struggling to get a foothold in the theater here in New York. She got a small part in a Broadway play and skyrocketed. Carleton got nowhere in particular; summer stock, an occasional TV commercial. She went to Hollywood and hit the moon. She was instantly in the center of all the stars, the glamor, the madness. Carleton followed her out there and they made some kind of effort to make it together. I think she tried, but too many famous men were camped on her trail. She was addicted to sex like a drug. Enormous vitality, enormous charm, enormous skills developed in the art of lovemaking. She could call her shots, pick her partners. There was no place in this new life for Carleton. They were divorced and she settled a solid chunk of money on him. Then she went her own delightful way."

"Now she's in her fifties," Ruysdale said.

"Fifty-one," Chambrun said. "Prime of life, in my book." He gave Ruysdale a wicked little smile. "Rich, famous, sought after, but uncertain. Were men after her because she was an irresistible woman, or because she was famous and rich? Was she still the greatest thing on wheels in bed, or was she just a series of notches on the handles of a series of guns? Were a new generation of men in Hollywood laughing at her for still having round heels?''

"Wasn't there a very young man a while back?'' Ruysdale asked.

Chambrun nodded. "Big to-do at the time,'' he said. "Big star takes on a kid twenty-five years her junior. She went public with it, too. They appeared together everywhere. She allowed herself to be interviewed on the subject of older women–younger men. Older men have been involved with much younger women for centuries, why not the reverse? There was a lot of snide gossip, of course. Victor Lewis—that was the boy's name—was just a paid gigolo; Sharon was a sex-crazy nymphomaniac, buying herself a young stud.''

"And the truth?'' Ruysdale asked.

Chambrun glanced at her. "I have an opinion, of course,'' he said. "She brought Vic Lewis east with her about four years ago. She came here to see a play she thought of buying as a film vehicle for herself. They stayed here at the hotel, of course. He spent part of an evening with me in the penthouse while she talked business with some bankers who might finance her project. Nice boy, clean-cut, angry at all the talk about them. He was, I thought, genuinely in love with her. He had a job at one of the big studios, determined to learn enough about the business aspects of the film industry to be able to handle her career somewhere up along the way. I was convinced he was no rip-off artist just feeding off a vain older woman. It wasn't his fault she was rich and famous. He loved her. Period.''

"So what happened to break it up?'' I seemed to remember something but I couldn't recall exactly what it was.

"About six months after that visit here Vic Lewis disappeared," Chambrun said.

"How do you mean, disappeared?"

"He just didn't come home one night. No word to Sharon. No explanation. His clothes, all his belongings, were at her home in Beverly Hills. He never came for them or sent for them. He never showed up at his job. The world thought he had just walked out on her. Sharon never believed that for a moment. If he'd had it with her, he'd have told her. She was certain he was too decent and honest a guy just to take a powder. They'd had no problems. Their love life, she told me later, was magical. So—she reported him to the police as a missing person. They turned up nothing. She spent a small fortune on private detectives who tried to trace him without any luck. Victor Lewis just vanished into thin air."

"And you think?" Ruysdale asked.

"Could have been an accident of some sort," Chambrun said. "Body not identified. He was fond of sailing and had a small boat Sharon had bought him. He could have drowned—except his boat was anchored at its mooring with no indication of any trouble."

"He could, of course, have done the one thing she didn't believe he could do—walk out on her. Alive and well and living in Paris," I said.

"Professional experts looked for him," Chambrun said. "It occurred to me he could have met with a violence; some former lover of Sharon's who wanted him out of the way, out of her life. She waited two years, living like a nun she tells me, for the smallest clue to what had become of him. The cops and the private detectives threw in the towel. Every time the phone rang

she felt a surge of hope. It was never Vic Lewis or anyone with news of him. Oh, there were some vicious
crackpots who hoped to earn the reward money she'd
posted. Nothing real."

"Rough on her," I said.

"Hellish for her," Chambrun said. "A year ago,
starved for what had been the core of her life—physical, sensual love—she finally took on another man—
another boy, twenty-five years her junior." Chambrun shrugged. "It was a formula that had worked so
well for her. But this one—Ted Valentine, a young actor in one of her films—was no Vic Lewis. Sexually he
is apparently a giant, but not tender and loving and
concerned as Vic Lewis was. They scream and fight and
yell at each other, and then forgive each other in bed.
He came here with her on this trip."

"I don't remember his being registered," I said.

"She rented a suite," Chambrun said. "It's like
subletting an apartment. If she wants to have a guest,
she's entitled. Last night he was to meet her in the Blue
Lagoon. They'd apparently had a fight about something earlier in the day. He threatened to walk out on
her—'just as Vic Lewis did.' When he didn't show up,
left her hanging in the Blue Lagoon, she blew her stack.
Teddy-boy was making public fun of her." Chambrun
crushed out his cigarette in the ashtray on his desk and
lit a fresh one. "When you persuaded her to go back
to her suite, Mark, she was half hopeful, half afraid
she'd find Valentine there, ready to pick up the fight.
What she found was worse, as far as she's concerned.
He was gone, his clothes gone, his belongings gone.
He'd done what he'd threatened to do—walked out on
her. The whole world would be laughing at her. The
fading movie star couldn't give her young lovers what

they needed. Now two of them had publicly given her the gate."

"This one just packed up and left," I said. "A little different from the first one, who disappeared leaving everything behind him."

Chambrun's eyes were narrowed in that "hanging judge" look I've mentioned. "I'd like to find this son-ofabitch and rub his nose in his own mess," he said. "And I'd like to find him before four o'clock this afternoon."

"Why the time limit?" I asked.

"Because Sharon Brand is scheduled to be a guest on the Dick Thomas show this afternoon," Chambrun said. "If I know Dick Thomas, one of the questions he'll ask her is about her much-publicized older woman-younger man relationships. God knows how she'll react when that happens. I tried to persuade her to ask Thomas to re-schedule her for later in the week. Maybe she and Teddy-boy will have made it up by then; at least she will have gotten hold of herself. She refused. You know how it is; the show must go on. She's given her word; her appearance has been advertised. A professional of her stature doesn't fail to meet her obligations."

"So how do I find Teddy-boy?" I asked.

"No one walks out of this hotel with luggage without paying a bill or having an adequate explanation," Chambrun said. "Somebody talked to him when he started to move out with his stuff. How did he explain it? Did he take a taxi? If he did, the doorman may remember. If it was a cab from the hackstand out front, the driver may remember where he took him. Do what you can, Mark. I don't want to see Sharon make an idiot of herself before millions of people. In a crazy

world her life style has been a touch unconventional,
but she doesn't deserve public ridicule.''

"On my way," I said.

YOU WOULDN'T BELIEVE the state of things in the
Beaumont's lobby that morning. If you have ever been
in the hotel at normal times, you'll know that the high-
ceilinged lobby has an almost cathedral calm and quiet.
If you choose to have a conversation of an intimate
nature with someone, you keep your voice down to
avoid being overheard. The hotel guests, the people
who came in out of the city to patronize the bars, the
restaurants, the meeting rooms, or to attend private
parties, are, by and large, conservatively and expensively dressed. It is a bastion against all the noise and
clamor of the outside world. You come through the
revolving doors from the street and into a completely
relaxed atmosphere. Look even slightly bewildered and
there is instantly someone at your elbow to offer directions, information, any assistance you need.

Not today.

Today it looked like the Woodstock rock festival,
hundreds of young people in jeans with long hair and
beards and beads! They jostled each other and shrieked
at friends on the other side of the lobby. It was bedlam, and it would get worse any minute when some famous guests of the Dick Thomas Show appeared for
rehearsal. Survival would depend on how gracious
those guests were in response to demands for autographs.

The kids in this crowd made most of the noise, but
there was a healthy percentage of older men and
women, some really old people. Many of them carried

their lunches in brown paper bags. In the Beaumont, for God sake!

Security was a massive headache and would get worse. In the corridors of the lobby were shops, men's and women's clothes, boutiques, gift shops, a bookstore, a drugstore. The unruly mob in the lobby weren't customers, but left unchecked, they would swarm into these places, handle the merchandise, turn the shops into a shambles. Jerry Dodd, our security chief, had taken on a couple of dozen outside professional guards to augment his own staff. These extras were mainly assigned to guard the shops.

The biggest problem created by the Dick Thomas Show was that the fifteen hundred people who could be wedged into the ballroom to watch the live show at four o'clock were dealt with on a first-come-first-served basis. Already, at ten in the morning, the corridors outside the Grand Ballroom were jammed wall to wall. Those people would have to wait at least five hours before the doors were opened. Gradually, backing up behind them, would be hundreds of people who would never get in, but hoping against hope that by some miracle there would be a place for them. The sight of the people jammed in ahead of them didn't seem to suggest that they might as well give up and try again some other time.

I saw Jerry Dodd standing two or three steps up the staircase that leads to the mezzanine and the Trapeze Bar. From there he could look out over the sea of screeching people. Jerry is an ex-FBI agent, bribed away by Chambrun some years ago to handle the hotel's security. He is a short, thin, wiry man with a hard, angular face. He is deceptive to people who don't know him. I've seen him handle a two-hundred-and-fifty-

pound professional football player like a helpless rag
doll. I think Jerry and Betsy Ruysdale and I are the
people on the staff closest to Chambrun. The maitre
d's in the restaurants and bars know their own depart-
ments, the people on the desk and the business office
know theirs, the bellhops, the porters, the chef, the
waiters, the telephone operators, the housekeepers,
many others all know theirs. Jerry and I touch all the
bases along with Ruysdale and The Man. We are a sort
of special family within the family.

"Looks like a breakout from a home for the men-
tally disturbed," Jerry said as I joined him on the
stairway. "What the hell does Dick Thomas have that
sucks them in?"

"The magic of show business," I said.

"Robert Redford ought to sue him for looking
alike," Jerry said.

"Sharon Brand is due to appear today," I said.
"Every movie buff in the country would like to see her
in the flesh, touch her, get her autograph."

"Which brings you to why you are here," Jerry said,
his thin lips twisted in a bitter little smile. "The boss
has already asked me the questions you're here to ask.
Nobody appears to have seen Teddy-boy Valentine
leave here last night with his luggage. He wasn't registered, so he didn't have to stop at the desk. None of my
people saw anyone trying to take off with luggage. The
four-to-midnight shift was on the bellhop schedule,
Mike Maggio in charge. He's doing overtime here this
morning to help out Johnny Thacker's crew. No one
was called to take luggage down from Fourteen B last
night. Mike was covering the lobby himself most of the
evening. He knows Ted Valentine by sight. Didn't see
him coming, going, circulating—nothing. I wonder

what Sharon Brand sees in him? She's a class lady and he's a jerk.''

"The magic chemistry of sex," I said.

"You're full of magic today. She can pretty well have the pick of the field. Anything wrong with picking a nice guy?"

"What makes you think he's a jerk?" I asked.

"Come on, Mark! You've been in this business long enough to smell a phony the minute one comes in off the street. You talked to Teddy-boy?"

"They only got here Saturday," I said. "It just happens I never laid eyes on him."

"He treats servants like servants, which is jerky," Jerry said. "Red carpet for the lady so there must be a red carpet for him. An insufferable prick, for my money. You can tell the lady for me she doesn't know how lucky she is."

"What I've got to try to do is to persuade Dick Thomas to delay Sharon's appearance on the show till later in the week. Maybe she and Teddy-boy will have kissed and made up by then."

"For her sake I hope he got run over by a truck," Jerry said.

MIKE MAGGIO, the night bell captain, was, as Jerry Dodd had told me, helping out the beleaguered day crew that morning. Mike—an Italian father and an Irish mother—is a character, an original; witty, mischievous, marvelously efficient at his job. He knows how to charm an Arab sheik or your maiden aunt from Peoria. He is one of the shrewdest judges of people I know. Someday, I think, he may wind up running his own hotel.

"I don't miss much around here, Mark," he said when I caught up with him. He and a couple of Jerry's extra guards were patrolling the banks of elevators to keep the Thomas fans from swarming into the upper regions of the hotel. "It was quiet here last night, you know? Normal." He made a wry face at the lobby mob. "I couldn't spot my own mother in that bunch. But last night was normal. I know Ted Valentine by sight—unfortunately. I brace myself when I see him because I expect some kind of trouble from him."

"Jerry gave me the impression that he's not loved."

"Not loved by anyone except that fabulous lady," Mike said. "They came in Saturday night, you know? Mr. Chambrun had alerted me, so I was ready to handle their luggage and get them to Fourteen B. She remembered me from other visits. She was warm and lovely. He was his rotten self. He treats anyone who's there to serve him like a galley slave. And tips?" Mike grinned. "He makes the original John D. Rockefeller and his dimes look like a philanthropist. Miss Brand knows what a cheapskate he is and always sweetens the pot when he isn't looking. But to get back to your problems."

"Do that chum," I said. "I'm running out of time."

"Last night, you know? Miss Brand turned up in the lobby about nine o'clock. I saw her and asked if I could do anything for her. She said she had a table reserved in the Blue Lagoon. Had I seen Mr. Valentine anywhere? He was supposed to join her. I hadn't. Well, if I saw him, would I tell him she was in the Lagoon. But I didn't see him, you know?"

"You off the floor much?" I asked him.

"Quiet Sunday," Mike said. "We're full up, you know? Nobody coming in with luggage to be handled.

Only three or four checkouts, no one I had to handle personally—except for my famous smile.'' He made a funny face. ''I was in and out of the drugstore a couple of times. Iverson, on the desk, had a headache and I got him some Bufferin. Some guy in Twelve H found he hadn't packed his razor. I bought him a Trac Two and sent it up by one of the boys. I went to the men's room a couple of times for personal reasons. Most of the time just talking with people I know, the people who were coming and going from the main dining room, the Trapeze, the Spartan Room. About ten o'clock one of Cardoza's boys came out with a message from Miss Brand. Would I go up to her suite and see if Mr. Valentine was there, tell him she was waiting for him.''

''You went up?''

''Of course. No answer when I rang the doorbell, so I let myself in with a pass key. I thought his nibs might just be sulking, not answering. He wasn't there.''

''You looked in his room?''

''I looked in all the rooms. The night maid doesn't come through to turn down the beds till about ten-thirty. She hadn't been there yet.''

''Did you look in his closets?''

''Hell, no. Why should I? I went back downstairs and told Cardoza to tell the lady he wasn't up there. I hadn't seen him.''

''So you don't know if his clothes were gone then?''

''Had no reason to look. About eleven the lady started throwing things in the Lagoon and using unladylike language. It didn't occur to me that Teddy-boy had checked out. He had two big suitcases when he came. If he'd walked out with them while I was off the floor, he'd have been noticed.''

"He should have been, but he wasn't," I said.

Mike shrugged. "I suppose. But I have to believe that, unless he went out the window, he left before I came on duty at five. I asked Johnny Thacker. He didn't see him."

"Just one of those things that shouldn't happen but did," I said.

"If he was trying to get out unnoticed, he could have tried the freight elevator and one of the basement exits," Mike said.

The basement isn't exactly the catacombs. There are the kitchens, the storage rooms, the utility areas. It's not deserted. All kinds of help in the kitchens, the chief engineer and a couple of his assistants always on duty. It would be a miracle if someone could wander around down there with a couple of suitcases and not be noticed. If he'd been noticed, it would have been reported. The disappearance of Teddy-boy began to take on all the elements of a mystery, but solving it wasn't my problem just then. I had to try to persuade Dick Thomas to get Sharon Brand to delay her appearance on his show till Valentine turned up and she got back on the rails again.

If you knew how, there were a couple of ways to get to the Grand Ballroom without fighting your way through the army of Dick Thomas fans wedged in front of the main entrance. I chose to go up to the mezzanine and down a back stairway that took me into the dressing room area behind the ballroom stage.

The orchestra was already out on stage in a rehearsal setup. I could hear Jake Floyd's restless fingers at the piano, waiting for some kind of cue. I moved into the wings where I could see out onto the stage. The orchestra, shirt-sleeved, wasn't dressed for the show. Jake Floyd at the piano spotted me and his head jerked up and down so that the ever-present cigar in the corner of his mouth seemed to point at me, a signal of greeting.

Unless you've been backstage or even a member of the audience during a show, you can't imagine what a jungle of cables, lights, cameras, standing and hand microphones it is. On the opposite side of the wings from where I stood was the glassed-in control booth where the director, Tony Meador, a bald genius at this kind of thing, handled the show. He was working at the moment with a long-haired young man with a guitar hung around his neck. I recognized Buddy Sellers, one of the top country-and-western singers of the day.

"Come downstage a little farther, Buddy," the director was saying over his loudspeaker. "Another step or two. There! You're right in the light there. I'll have a stage manager give you a chalk mark on the floor."

A young man appeared from somewhere and made a chalk X on the floor at the singer's feet.

"Okay," Meador's voice came over the loudspeaker. "Now you go back out center. I'll read Dick's introductory speech, Jake and the boys will give you a lead-in, and you come straight out to that chalk mark. There'll be applause, a lot of it. Jake and the boys will keep vamping behind you till you raise your head. That'll be the signal for them to go into the intro. Clear?"

Buddy Sellers signaled "clear" and came back offstage. I didn't know him, but he winked at me. Meador's voice came over the loudspeaker again.

"And now, ladies and gentlemen, my next guest is a blah, blah, blah, who has six gold records and is riding the top of the country-and-western charts, a man

who, blah, blah, blah; a man who blah, blah, blah—
Buddy Sellers!"

Sellers bounded out onto the stage, carrying his guitar and a hand-mike with its cable trailing behind him. Jake and his boys played something lively.

"Applause, applause, applause, applause, applause," Meador was saying over his speaker.

Sellers reached the chalk mark, nodding and bowing to a nonexistent audience. Jake and the boys were vamping behind him. Then he raised his head and Jake shifted to the formal introduction to a number. Buddy began to sing.

Mamma, I gotta tell you it hurts.
Mamma, I gotta tell you it hurts.
Mamma, I gotta tell you it hurts.
It hurts, it hurts, it hurts.
Mamma, I gotta tell you it hurts,
Real bad—

I'm not much of a fan for this modern, so-called music; the lyrics repeated over and over, the same musical phrase repeated over and over. You get the idea after a while that something hurts! I turned away and came face to face with one of the assistant stage managers I knew from past years. We said hello and I asked him for Dick Thomas.

"He's in his dressing room," the guy said. "I don't think he can be disturbed right now. He's going over the day's material with Laura."

"Emergency," I said.

I moved across the backstage to the star's dressing room and knocked. After a moment the door opened and I found myself facing Laura Sayles, the Twiggy-type researcher I've mentioned. She stared at me through those huge, round glasses. It took seconds for her to put two and two together and come up with Mark Haskell.

"Oh, hi," she said.

"See Dick for a minute?" I asked.

"It's not a good time," she said.

"Emergency," I said.

She shrugged and stood aside.

Dick Thomas, coatless, tieless, was stretched out on a wicker chaise longue, a sheaf of notes on a little table beside him. He sat up when he saw me.

"Haskell! Long time no see," he said. He held out his hand and I went over to shake it, a nice firm, but not-too-firm, grip. He is so damned good-looking— blond hair nicely trimmed at a medium length, warm, gently amused blue eyes, good bones and a square jaw, chin with a dimple in the center of it, à la Kirk Douglas. His image is "Mr. Nice Guy," and maybe it's more than an image. He's been married to the same woman, who stays in the background, for more than twenty years, and has three teen-age kids—two girls and a boy. I guess he hasn't yet reached forty-five.

I glanced at Laura "Twiggy" Sayles. This flat-chested, goggled-eyed girl belongs to a special club: women who are in love with the boss and never make it. The way she looked at Dick Thomas, waiting for him to take charge, I was reminded of Buddy Sellers' song: "Mamma, I gotta tell you it hurts."

"How goes it, Mark?" Dick asked, smiling at me. "As I remember, you're always falling in love forever every few months. Who is she and how goes it?"

"I'm between innings at the moment," I said.

"Lot of real fancy dolls coming on this week," he said. "Maybe we can find you a candidate. Laura's briefing me on today's guests. What can I do for you?"

"Sharon Brand," I said.

"Oh, brother!" He leaned back on the chaise longue. "Chambrun called me about her, her wing ding last night in the Blue Lagoon. Ted Valentine hasn't shown up?"

"Not yet."

"I called her suite and offered her the opportunity to come on later in the week. No dice. She'd made her commitment. It's been advertised, *TV Guide*, the works. She's a pro. Her private life mustn't be allowed to interfere with her professional obligations."

"You planning to talk to her about her older woman-younger man syndrome?" I asked.

"That's what women want to hear," Dick said.

"If you'd seen her last night, you might decide not to risk it," I said.

"So Chambrun said."

"This is the second young stranger who's walked out on her," I said. "God knows what she'll have to say about the whole notion today. I think you should give her time, whether she wants it or not. Can't you shift some other big-time guest to today and have her later in the week when Teddy-boy's showed up or she's cooled off?"

"I'd like to," Dick said. "I urged her to shift. She won't. She's big-time stuff, Mark. I can't tell her I don't want her on. I'll just have to handle the chips the way they fall. I'll try to talk about her latest film, keep her off the touchy subject of young men."

The telephone on his dressing table rang, and Laura Sayles crossed the room to answer it.

"Mr. Haskell, it's for you," she said.

I wondered who knew I was here. Mike Maggio? Jerry Dodd? I took the phone from Laura. It was Betsy Ruysdale, The Man's secretary.

"Hang onto your hat, Mark," Ruysdale said.

"What's up?"

"You're wanted up here on the double," she said. "Teddy-boy has turned up."

"So, good," I said.

"Very dead," Ruysdale said.

"What the hell are you talking about?" I heard myself ask her.

The phone disconnected.

THREE

TED VALENTINE hadn't gone into the next world without knowing what hit him. Someone had confronted him head-on. His face had been mangled, his skull crushed in by someone who had faced him and beaten down on him, according to Lieutenant Hardy of Manhattan Homicide.

Lieutenant Hardy is an old friend of ours, particularly of Chambrun's, whom we meet from time to time, always under unhappy circumstances. As I have said, murders in the Beaumont were not unheard of; they happened here as they happen in any city. Hardy, a big blond man who looks more like a plodding fullback on a professional football team than anything else, is actually a very good and very thorough homicide detective. He and Chambrun have a way of complementing each other when they face a crime. Chambrun is intuitive, often jumping to a conclusion without checking the in-betweens; Hardy is slow, dogged, checking every facet of a case, and almost always coming out where Chambrun had arrived by his own special genius.

Ted Valentine had been found in an alley about a block east of the Beaumont. Whoever had beaten him to a pulp had removed every possible means of identification. There was no wallet, no money—not even change—no keys, no nothing. A kid, wandering up the alley in search of God knows what, had stumbled on the bloodied body and rushed out to find a cop on the beat. That had been about seven A.M., four and a half hours ago. The Medical Examiner's office made an educated guess that he'd been killed hours before that, probably early Sunday evening, about the time he should have been keeping his date with Sharon Brand in the Blue Lagoon. His fingerprints had produced no records in the local files or, so far, in the FBI records in Washington. They had an unidentified dead man.

But Hardy is Hardy. He observed that his victim was wearing a five-hundred-dollar Italian silk suit, a pair of hundred-and-fifty dollar custom-made shoes, a seventy-dollar white broadcloth shirt, and a silk tie that must have cost forty or fifty bucks. That kind of gear suggested the Beaumont to the Lieutenant—a guest of the hotel mugged as he walked to or from the place where he was staying. Only called onto the case when he had come to work this morning, Hardy, after reviewing the reports of the preliminary investigation, had called Mr. Atterbury on the front desk and asked him to come down to the morgue and have a look.

The face was too mutilated for Atterbury to be certain, but he knew from word around the hotel that Ted Valentine had been missing since last night, and the rest of the body's appearance, the clothes, fit his almost photographic memory of Sharon Brand's young man. A check with Los Angeles police nailed it down. Teddy-boy had been fingerprinted for some kind of civil defense operation out there.

Hardy was in Chambrun's office when I got there from Dick Thomas's dressing room. He and Chambrun brought me up to date.

"I'm going to have to talk to the lady," Hardy said. "It's probably just a particularly brutal mugging, but I have to check with her."

Chambrun sat huddled in the chair behind his desk, his eyes in their deep pouches narrowed against the smoke from his cigarette.

"No luggage?" he asked.

"Luggage?"

"He appears to have left the hotel with two large suitcases containing all his clothes and personal belongings which he'd had in his room in Miss Brand's suite," Chambrun said.

Hardy shrugged. "Extra loot for the mugger," he said.

"Your description, friend, suggests Valentine was pretty severely beaten," Chambrun said. "Face mutilated, skull crushed in."

"Nine or ten pretty savage blows, according to the Medical Examiner," Hardy said.

"Why would an ordinary mugger go crazy wild like that?" Chambrun asked. "He'd only have to hit him once or twice to knock him cold and strip him of his belongings. What you describe sounds like someone in a rage."

"Maybe Valentine fought back," Hardy suggested. "That could trigger some kind of psychotic violence."

"What about his hands?"

"What about his hands?"

"If he put up a fight, there should be some kind of marks on his hands, shouldn't there? Maybe something under his fingernails where he gouged at his attacker?"

Hardy looked steadily at The Man. "Nothing like that," he said slowly. "The M.E. checked, thinking the mugger might be marked when we catch up with him."

Chambrun reached out and crushed his cigarette in the brass ashtray on his desk. "The Medical Examiner have any suggestions about the weapon used?"

"The proverbial blunt instrument," Hardy said. "He thinks metal. He found some flecks of rust in the wounds. Could have been a wrecking bar, or some kind of heavy metal wrench, even a hammer."

Chambrun lit a fresh cigarette with his gold lighter and took a deep drag on it. "I don't believe for an instant in your casual mugger, Hardy," he said.

"So, unconvince me," Hardy said, giving The Man a wry little smile.

"To start with, my track record," Chambrun said. "I have a feeling about it."

"And when you have a feeling—"

"Look, Hardy, I'd like it to be a mugger," Chambrun said. "I want it to be a mugger. A mugger wouldn't hurt our name here. An expensively dressed man, taking a casual stroll *outside* my hotel, a fairly obvious and profitable target for some drug-hungry punk. I'd like it that way. But the violence of the attack suggests he was waylaid, not just because he looked prosperous but because he was who he was— Ted Valentine. The removal of every scrap of identification from the body—why? A casual mugger doesn't give a hoot whether you identify the victim or not."

"A wallet with credit cards. Negotiable," Hardy said.

"And running down the street with two heavy suitcases? Not likely. The suitcases are gone, Hardy, with all his clothes, shoes, personal belongings."

"Stuff could be pawned or fenced," Hardy said. "Supply this guy, the mugger, with drugs for a long time. A rich haul for him."

Chambrun, stubborn, shook his head. "A little over two years ago a young man living with Sharon Brand disappeared from the face of the earth. Now we have another young man living with the lady. Except for your shrewd hunch that a man, dressed as he was, might be a guest of the Beaumont's, Ted Valentine might very well have, in effect, disappeared, too. A nameless corpse in the morgue. No, Hardy, the coincidence is too great. There's a pattern here that needs to be explored, and I'll give you odds the picture doesn't include a mugger when it's put together."

Hardy was silent for a moment, looking thoughtfully at Chambrun. Chambrun's hunches had paid off for him on other occasions. "I guess it's an angle that has to be checked," he said finally. "Which means I have to talk to Sharon Brand. Who were Valentine's friends, his enemies?"

"Who are *her* enemies?" Chambrun said. "I'd like you to give us the chance to break the news to her about Valentine before you ask her questions. She has a right to a chance to get herself pulled together."

"Be my guest," Hardy said. "Set up a time for me—in an hour, say?"

"I'll do my best," Chambrun said. He reached for the phone on his desk and asked to be connected with Fourteen B. He threw the switch on the squawk box so that we'd all hear the conversation. Sharon Brand's voice came through, firm and clear.

"Pierre here," Chambrun said. "I'd like to come up and see you, Sharon."

"I'm due for a briefing with Dick Thomas in half an hour," Sharon said. "Would after that do, Pierre?"

"I think not," Chambrun said. "I have some news about Ted Valentine."

"You've located the sonofabitch?" she asked, her voice harsh.

"I know where he is, Sharon," The Man said. "I'd prefer not to talk about it over the switchboard phone."

"I've got to leave in twenty minutes for the ballroom," she said.

"On my way," Chambrun said. He put down the phone and switched off the squawk box. "I think I'd like you to come with me, Mark. She's apt to hold together better with someone she doesn't know well there."

SHE GREETED US at the door of her suite, looking beautiful and youthful in a summer print dress, her blond hair hanging shoulder length, her bright blue eyes glittering with anger.

"Shacked up with whom?" she asked before either of us could speak.

Breaking the news that a lover has been brutally murdered isn't the easiest job. Chambrun chose to be tough about it.

"He's dead, Sharon," he said.

She started to reach out to him, and then straightened up and stood staring at us, rigid.

"Let's not talk about it out here in the hall," Chambrun said.

She turned and walked back through the vestibule and into the living room. I saw her fists were clenched together so tightly the knuckles were white. She stood in the center of the room, her back to us, waiting for Chambrun to go on.

"The police think it may have been a mugger," Chambrun said. "He was found in an alley about a block from the hotel, beaten to death, robbed."

"Oh my God!" she said. It was a whisper.

"Before we talk about it, Sharon, I think we should call Dick Thomas and tell him you can't appear on his show today," Chambrun said.

"It's a professional commitment," she said, her back still to us. "I have to keep it."

"This is going to be all over the radio and television and in the evening paper before show time," Chambrun said. "There's no way you can go on the show today without millions of people gawking at you and wondering how you could be so unfeeling about a man you were publicly living with."

She turned, slowly, to look at us. Her face looked as if a frozen mask had been drawn over it. I thought she couldn't move her lips to speak. Chambrun turned to me.

"Call Dick Thomas and tell him why Sharon can't appear today," he said.

"No!" Sharon said.

"He'll call you, love, when he hears the news," Chambrun said. "He wouldn't want to be in this situation with an interview. He couldn't ignore it, and he surely wouldn't want to talk about it."

She turned away and sank down in a corner of the couch. She had conceded. I went to the extension in the kitchenette and called Dick Thomas. It took a while, and some argument with his people, to get through to him. I told him what had happened. He was shocked.

"My God, we were set up to talk about that relationship," he said.

"Not today. Maybe not this week at all," I said. "She's sorry. She feels obligated, but—"

"I couldn't handle it," he said. "Tell her—my sympathy—whatever."

So much for Mr. Nice Guy.

Chambrun had taken an armchair facing Sharon when I rejoined them. He had obviously given her the bloody details. She was holding together with a kind of grim courage.

"The Dick Thomas Show isn't exactly my lucky charm," she said as I came in.

"How do you mean?" Chambrun asked her.

"It was two years and seven months ago," she said. "Dick was doing his show from Hollywood. I was on. The first time I'd talked about this older woman-younger man thing. It was that night that Vic disappeared. Victor Lewis, my man. You know all about it, Pierre. He just never came home—then or ever."

"The day you were on the Dick Thomas Show?" Chambrun asked, his eyes narrowed.

"No connection, of course," she said. "But that—and now this, the day I am scheduled to be on the show. Coincidence deluxe."

"If it is a coincidence," Chambrun said very quickly.

I could almost hear the wheels turning. He hadn't believed in a mugger from the start. Now Sharon had presented him with a link between two possible violences. Ted Valentine, beaten to death, stripped of all identification, hopefully to become a nameless corpse in the morgue; thirty-one months ago Vic Lewis had vanished, possibly the victim of another violence. Beware young lovers with a yen for an older glamor girl—who just happens to be going on the Dick Thomas

Show. Not very sensible, but I was sure that's what Chambrun was thinking.

"Poor Ted," Sharon said. "I don't think he was serious, but he used to say that probably some man out of my past would have at him someday."

"Who out of your past is connected with the Dick Thomas Show?" Chambrun asked.

She stared at him for a moment. There have been so many men in her life, I thought, that she had to stop to think.

"No one," she said finally.

"Positive?"

"My dear Pierre, of course I'm positive. You think I don't remember who my lovers have been?"

"Is there someone in the past," he asked, "who could be jealous enough of the present to go after Vic Lewis and then his successor?"

"That's absurd, Pierre." But she looked startled, thinking back.

"Did Valentine carry around a key to this suite?" Chambrun asked.

"He had a key, but I assume he would leave it at the desk if he went out somewhere. The keys have big tags on them, Pierre. A woman can carry one handily in her bag, but they're awkward for a man to carry in a pocket—bulky."

"He didn't leave his key at the desk," Chambrun said.

"Walking out with all his things," she said, bitterness creeping in. "I don't suppose he cared about the key."

"Maybe he didn't walk out with all his things," Chambrun said.

Her eyes widened. "He took all his clothes, everything."

"Maybe not," Chambrun said.

"I don't understand what you're getting at, Pierre."

"He had his key when he was attacked," Chambrun said. "He was stripped of everything. Wallet, money, everything; the key if he was carrying it. Then, whoever attacked him, took the key, let himself in up here while you were in the Blue Lagoon, and took all of Valentine's clothes and possessions."

"That just doesn't make sense," she said after a moment of dead silence. "I have a hundred thousand dollars' worth of jewelry in a box on my bureau. Nothing touched. I've just been through it, trying to decide what to wear on Dick's show. A thief wouldn't have overlooked that. Ted had expensive clothes, but nothing much else of value. He wore a gold watch I bought him in Switzerland, a Chinese jade ring I bought him for his birthday. If someone was robbing the place, he wouldn't have overlooked my things."

"You don't put your jewelry in the hotel safe?"

"No, I don't," she said. "It's insured. I don't want to have to run up and down stairs every time I want a different ring, or bracelet, or pin, or necklace..."

"I asked you about someone from the past who might want to hurt you," Chambrun said. "What could hurt you most in this world, Sharon?" When she didn't answer, he went on. "What would hurt you most would be to have a man walk out on you. Maybe someone wanted it to look that way."

"Pierre!"

"A theory that needs looking into," he said. He stood up. "Lieutenant Hardy of Homicide is going to

have to talk to you, Sharon. I suggest you get it over
with now. I'll send him up. Mark will stay with you so
you won't feel left to the wolves.''

HE LEFT US, me with my head spinning a little. The
Man had put together about as far-out a notion as I
could imagine. It seemed totally unlikely to me, but he
had a way of coming out of left field with the impossible that would prove to be right.

"He's quite out of his mind, isn't he?" Sharon
asked. She hadn't moved from her corner of the couch,
staring at the door Chambrun had closed behind him
when he left.

"He has a tantalizing way of hitting the target from
around a corner," I said.

She stood up. "It's a little early in the day, but since
I'm not going on Dick's show I think I could do with a
drink. How about you? Name your poison."

"Jack Daniel's, or any other bourbon, on the
rocks—if you have it."

"Teddy drank Jack Daniel's," she said, and headed
for the kitchenette.

I stood where I was, listening to the sound of ice
cubes feeding out of the ice-maker. A man out of the
past; a rejected lover? Some connection with the Dick
Thomas Show, or was that just a coincidence? Coincidence, I knew, was a dirty word in Chambrun's book.

Sharon reappeared with my Jack Daniel's and what
looked like a vodka and tonic for herself. She held out
her glass to touch mine and we drank a little. She went
back to the couch and sat there looking at me. It's an
odd thing about finding yourself in the company of a
stranger that you've seen on the screen all your life. I
felt as if Sharon was an old friend.

"You must wonder about me," she said after a moment.

I tried the Haskell charm on her. "I think I've been a little bit in love with you ever since I was in knee pants," I said.

"I don't care to be reminded of how long it's been," she said.

"At least thirty years," I said. "You were in a film with George Brent, and I was shot down, right between the eyes."

"At age six?" she said.

"Approximately," I said. "It started me on a roller-coaster ride I've never been able to get off. Falling in love forever, over and over again."

She gave me a thoughtful look, and I had the feeling I had dropped into place in some private computer of hers. "There is nothing so exciting as falling in love," she said. "More exciting than a great film role, more exciting than the applause of a Broadway audience after a performance in a play that really came off."

"It's the top," I said, quoting Cole Porter. " '—it's the tower of Pisa, it's the smile on the Mona Lisa.' "

She smiled, and then her face clouded over. "This detective who's coming to question me, what kind of questions will he have, Mark?"

"Mostly about Valentine, I imagine. Lieutenant Hardy is a good cop, very thorough, but very sensitive to what he knows you must be feeling."

"Do you have any idea what I am feeling, Mark?" she asked. Her bright blue eyes looked past me to something far away, I thought.

"Shock, loss," I said.

"Shock, yes," she said. "Violence against any human being shocks me. Loss, no."

I remembered her the night before, beating at the pillows on the couch and cursing Teddy-boy. "That miserable bastard walked out on me," she'd told me, told Chambrun. It had seemed like a deep, cutting loss to me at the time.

"You're thinking about the scene I played last night in the Blue Lagoon, and later up here with you and Pierre," she said. "Rejected woman, enraged, grief-stricken."

"If it wasn't real, it was a great act," I said.

"Oh, it was real enough—the rage part of it," she said. "You see, Mark, Teddy and I had come to the end of the line. We both knew it. But *I* had the right to make the public move that would end it—after all I'd done for him, given him. *I* had the right to make the move so that the whole damn world wouldn't be suddenly laughing at me. We'd talked about it quite calmly. He'd given up almost a year of his life to me. I was quite willing to take care of his financial problems until he got reorganized. *But I had the right to make the move out!*" Her voice rose, and I had a flash of the fierce anger I'd seen last night. "Loss, no; it was already over. Maybe I should be grateful to him that he got himself killed. No one will be laughing at me now."

I guess I felt something like shock at that moment. That was about as cold-blooded as you could get, I thought. And yet I understood it in a way. The great sex symbol of the last thirty years, walked out on by a young lover, would be laughed at by a segment of her huge public, the subject of bawdy jokes in men's rooms, and in the circles of women who had been jealous and envious of her all her career. No one would

dare express anything but sympathy for the violent end
to her affair with Teddy-boy. No one would dare suggest that, at fifty-one, she couldn't satisfy a lover
young enough to be her son.

I didn't have to comment, because the doorbell rang
and I knew it would be Lieutenant Hardy. I stopped at
the door as I went to open it.

"I think what you've just told me should be between you and me and Mr. Chambrun," I said. "If
some smart-assed reporter got hold of it—"

HARDY WAS EVERYTHING I'd promised Sharon he
would be, thorough in trying to build up a dossier on
Ted Valentine, not pressing her, letting what she knew
come out as she chose to feed it to him.

Teddy Valentine had been twenty-six years old, born
and raised here in New York. His parents, with assistance supplied by Sharon, had retired to Florida. She
had never met them. They hadn't approved of their
son's relationship with an older woman, but they'd
evidently been willing enough to take her money.
Teddy-boy had gone to a high school in the Bronx, but
no college that he'd ever mentioned to Sharon. Hardy
suggested that he might have friends—or enemies—
here in the city that he might have mentioned. Not to
her, according to Sharon.

He had come into her life in California. It had been
a rough time for her. Vic Lewis had been missing for
more than a year when she first met Teddy. He had
done some technical work in television here in the city,
camera crew on industrial shows, and when jobs
thinned out, he'd gone to Hollywood where television
was flourishing. Sharon was still stubbornly spending
a fortune on private investigators in the hope of find-

ing some trace of Vic Lewis. Her story was no secret. Before Lewis vanished she'd been public about her older woman-younger man setup.

Before she went very far with the story, I got the feeling that Sharon had been stalked by a scheming jerk. Teddy-boy was handsome, physically attractive, and out for himself. He managed to meet her on the set of a film she was making. He'd gotten a job at the studio as an extra. He was sympathetic, flattering, playing on what was a long period, for her, of no sex, no romance. She finally toppled.

"He wasn't Vic Lewis," she told Hardy. "Vic was tender, loving, sensitive to my needs, my professional as well as personal problems. A perfect companion. I had been prepared to spend the rest of my life with him—if he'd kept on wanting me. Teddy was a massive ego, selfish, demanding—really not a very nice guy. But he was a marvelous lover. I needed that when he came along. But after we'd been together for a while I knew that it could only be temporary." Her laugh was brittle. "I didn't really like him, you see. He was a first-class heel, greedy for all the things I could give him— luxury, some sort of social status in the movie world. I could get him jobs, which he didn't keep. He paid for everything—in bed."

Hardy looked embarrassed. "He got along with your friends?" he asked.

That mask-like look seemed to harden her face. "I don't have friends, Lieutenant," she said. "Oh, there are people who fawn over me, crowd around me, try to fill up my time. I'm surrounded by people, but not friends. It's gone on for so long that way—people want from me. Can't you guess why there have been so many men in my life, Lieutenant?"

"Because you are a beautiful woman," Hardy said.

"Thank you, Lieutenant, but that's not it. To make love to a famous, glamorous, international sex symbol is a great ego-builder. I have only been sure twice in my life that a man really loved me for what I am, the person I am, and not just an opportunity to bolster his masculinity. Vic Lewis, very late in my life, was one of those two I was sure of, and now, unless I find out what happened to him, I can't even be sure of that. The other was my husband—thirty-two years ago before I was anyone. A nice, stupid boy who thought I was a nice, stupid girl. After that I settled for virility and didn't ask for anything else, because I could never be sure."

"And that ex-husband, Miss Brand?" Hardy asked.

She gave a brittle laugh. "Thirty-odd years, Lieutenant. Would you believe I can't really remember clearly what he looked like? I might not know him if I passed him on the street—after thirty years."

"There's no way he could forget how you look, Miss Brand, your face on screens everywhere, in magazines, on posters."

"Why should it matter to him after all this time?"

"Women friends?" Hardy asked.

"Women see me as dangerous competition, and I am," Sharon said. She hesitated. "There is one man I think of as a friend, perhaps because he has never made a pass at me. He has listened to my woes, advised me, helped me, but never once made a move in my direction. Strangely enough, I trust him for that very reason. I'm talking about Pierre Chambrun."

"A good friend to have," Hardy said. He glanced at his notes. "He has a pretty wild theory about this."

"I know," Sharon said.

"Victor Lewis disappeared a day when you were on the Dick Thomas Show in California—three years ago?"

"Two years and seven months," Sharon said. I expected her to add something like "six hours and eight minutes." She kept that close to that past.

"And you were due to go on the Dick Thomas Show today?"

"Yes."

"Do you see any connection between the two things—Mr. Lewis's disappearance and the murder of Ted Valentine?"

"What possible connection could there be? It's just a grim throw of the dice that doesn't have any meaning."

"Maybe," Hardy said.

Sharon's eyes widened. "You see some connection?"

"I at least want to prove that there is none," Hardy said.

I knew Hardy. He would worry at it and worry at it until he proved there was no connection, or he would find that there was and bring it out into the open, screaming for mercy. He wouldn't let go. Not Hardy.

"I find it a little awkward to ask you about—about the men in your life, Miss Brand," he said.

"So don't ask," she said sharply. "The publishing business is getting rich today on books by ladies who write about their love affairs with famous men. Kiss-and-tell garbage, I call them. Not me, Lieutenant. Not for profit, not for gossip, not for the police!"

"Not even if one of them was responsible for the disappearance of Victor Lewis and the murder of Ted Valentine?" he asked.

"You surely don't believe that!"

"I don't believe anything yet, Miss Brand. About the Dick Thomas Show—that grim throw of the dice you mentioned. What is your relationship to Dick Thomas?"

She laughed. "Do you know what they call him in the business, Lieutenant? Mr. Nice Guy! He's been married to the same woman for twenty-odd years, has three kids, is involved every day of his life with famous actresses, singers, dancers, lady comics. And when the day's work is done he goes home to a nice home-cooked dinner. I've never heard a whisper about him. I can promise you he never looked my way except to ask me well-prepared questions on camera."

"You've been on his show often?"

"Four times—this was to have been the fifth. That covers a stretch of fifteen—eighteen years, Lieutenant. We aren't close. We get along very well professionally."

"Anyone else on his show? Other men? Some jealous woman?"

"I don't really know anyone except Laura Sayles, who researches Dick's guests for him. She always interviews me before he goes on the air, prepares his questions for him. The rest of his crew—some of them have been with him a long time—are just faces. I smile and say hello, and that's that."

Hardy hesitated. "Did Valentine have friends on the Thomas staff? People he might have worked with in the past? Camera crews were his thing, you said. Some girl on the staff with whom he might have been intimate before—before—"

"Before Sharon Brand?" she asked, with that bitter little smile.

"Yes, ma'am," Hardy said.

"Teddy never mentioned knowing anyone on the show, male or female," she said. "Dick Thomas's camera people have been with him for years. I don't believe there's a chance Teddy ever worked with any of them anywhere else. As for women, your guess is as good as mine, Lieutenant. He wouldn't have thought it was healthy to mention other women to me."

"Victor Lewis—did he know people on the Thomas Show?"

Just the mention of Vic Lewis's name brought about a change in Sharon. Her face softened, the color of her eyes seemed to deepen. She had loved the guy, I thought. The hurt of losing him two years and seven months ago cut deeper than the violent dispatching of Teddy-boy today.

"Vic made a point of knowing people with whom I was professionally involved," she said. "We both thought that someday he would be my manager. We both wanted it. That day—the day he disappeared—he was supposed to be at the studio where Dick Thomas was televising his show. He didn't show. He didn't call, which was unlike him. He just—just vanished. I think he knew a lot of the people who worked for Dick Thomas."

"But he hadn't become your manager or agent," Hardy said.

"It was just ahead, just around the corner," Sharon said.

"Who does manage your career for you, Miss Brand?"

"Ray Baxter."

I didn't know if Hardy was aware that in Hollywood Ray Baxter is *the* top agent and manager of stars. He has a whole stable of them. I remembered Chambrun telling me that Sharon had been one of his first clients and that her meteoric career, quite possibly brilliantly handled by Baxter, had made him top dog in his field. I wondered, looking at her, if somewhere along the way Baxter had been one of her romances. Called "Red" by his friends because of his carrot-colored hair, Baxter was a notorious womanizer. I suspect that today, because of his professional genius, all Baxter had to do was beckon a new young starlet to get her into his loft.

"Is this Baxter here in New York to handle your appearance on the Dick Thomas Show?" Hardy asked.

"My dear Lieutenant," she said, laughing, "do you know what Dick Thomas pays for an appearance on his show? Five hundred dollars. Peanuts. The reason that people in my position go for it is that he promotes my newest film to a huge audience. It wouldn't be unreasonable if we paid him instead of vice versa. So you can see Red Baxter wouldn't fly to New York just to earn his ten percent of my five hundred dollars."

"How did Baxter feel about your relationship with Ted Valentine?" Hardy asked.

"Red handles my professional career, not my private life," she said.

"But he could have felt the relationship with Valentine was damaging to your career?"

The hard mask was in place again. "So he flies to New York, beats Teddy to death just to advance my career? I think I've heard enough absurdities from you and Pierre for one day, Lieutenant," she said.

Hardy slipped his notebook back in his pocket and stood up. "I'm going to need a formal statement from you, Miss Brand. The last time you saw Valentine, what his plans were, your plans. Details. I'd like to come back with a police stenographer in about an hour.

Meanwhile I'm going to station a man here in your suite.''

"Why on earth?" she asked.

He gave her a steady look. "We could have some kind of a psycho running around loose," he said. "There's just a chance you could be a target. Until I know more than I do now, I don't choose to take that chance."

"Me a target?" Her question suggested total disbelief.

"It isn't my wish to frighten you, Miss Brand," Hardy said. "But surely, after all the efforts of the Los Angeles police and your private detectives, you must be convinced that Victor Lewis, who loved you, who had a future with you, didn't just run away. I have to think he was murdered, and that the murderer was successful in doing away with the body."

"Oh, God!" she said.

"The murderer could have been someone who hated Victor Lewis, but it's equally possible that someone hated you and chose that way to hurt you. Now we have Valentine, the current man in your life, murdered. Maybe the murderer hated him, but it is just as possible that this was another attempt to hurt you. And next? If we have a person who hates you so much he will murder people you care for to hurt you, he may decide finally to attack you directly."

"That's madness!"

"Yes, isn't it?" Hardy said quietly. "Madness is why I intend to protect you, Miss Brand."

She drew a deep, shuddering breath and looked at me. Hardy had really meant to frighten her and he'd succeeded.

"I think I'd like to talk to Pierre," she said to me.

FOUR

MISS RUYSDALE told me that The Man was "circulating" when I tried to get him on the phone to tell him Sharon needed him. That meant he was checking out on how his world was rotating, probably seeing for himself how badly the Dick Thomas fan club in the lobby was disrupting things. Best thing I could do for Sharon was to go find him.

Hardy had gone to the front door of the suite, and he came back with a plainclothes cop whom he introduced as Sergeant Croft. He asked me to show Croft the layout, which included a rear door that leads out to the service area, the freight elevators, and the fire stairs. Croft bolted the door on the inside and then checked out the two bedrooms and the two baths, the kitchenette.

He reported back to Hardy. The sergeant was a man of few words. He had spoken about four to me as I'd taken him on the tour.

"All clear, Lieutenant," he said. "Service door bolted on the inside."

Hardy nodded and turned to Sharon, who had drawn that frozen mask over her face again. "Sergeant Croft will set himself up in the vestibule, Miss Brand," he said. "I have another man out in the front corridor. No one will be permitted in to see you without my permission except Mark here, Mr. Chambrun, and Jerry Dodd, who is the hotel's security officer. As I told you, I'll be back in about an hour with a stenographer to take a formal statement. Is there anything you need?"

"The answer to a question," she said in a flat, hard voice. "What will happen if I put on my hat, pick up my purse, walk out of here and take the next plane back to my home in California?"

"Sergeant Croft has orders to arrest you, place you in protective custody, if you try anything like that, Miss Brand. I think you'd find a cell in a city jail a lot harder to take than this suite. I'm not through with you yet, Miss Brand. I hope when I am you'll have abandoned any such notion and let us protect you."

"I'll find Mr. Chambrun as quickly as I can," I told her.

We left her standing there like a marble statue. I don't suppose anyone had given her orders for the last thirty years. She was the queen in her world.

Out in the main corridor Hardy spoke to another plainclothes cop who was there, and then we walked to the elevators together.

"You really think she's in danger?" I asked him.

"If I ignored the possibility and anything happened to her, I wouldn't want to look in my shaving mirror in the morning," Hardy said. "I saw what is left of Teddy Valentine. It isn't pretty, Mark."

I felt a little tingle of apprehension run along my spine. Between them Chambrun and Hardy had evidently made me a believer.

Downstairs there was a new dimension to the lobby confusion. The press! They weren't there to cover the Dick Thomas Show. The news of the murder was out, and as Hardy and I got off the elevator they swarmed around us, a couple of dozen, I guess. Hardy was courteous but abrupt with them. It was too soon for

him to make any kind of statement. Yes, there had
been a murder. Yes, the victim was a man named Ted
Valentine who had been staying at the Beaumont. No,
there were no suspects, no leads yet.

"Was this Valentine Sharon Brand's latest boyfriend?"

"No comment."

"Is he *that* Valentine?"

"No comment."

"Why make it tough for us, Lieutenant?"

Hardy's smile was thin. "Find a way to make my job
easier for me and I might find a way to make your job
easier for you," he said, and took off.

That left me surrounded. I was having a slight personal problem. On the outer rim of this press group,
most of whom I knew, was a dark, trim, sexy-looking
doll I knew too damn well. She was Jody Powers, who
writes a syndicated gossip column, "Powers' House,"
which is read from one end of the country to the other.
Everybody who is anybody passes through the Beaumont at one time or another. It is the home-away-from-
home for top United Nations bigwigs, a hangout for
the so-called Beautiful People, a base for visiting Hollywood stars and the British acting greats who appear
on Broadway. All Jody had to do to fill her column
each day was to lunch at the Beaumont or turn up in
the Trapeze Bar at cocktail time and the people she
wanted to write about were there. She was a regular,
usually appearing, I regret to say, with some attrac-
tive-looking male escort.

Jody had had my appetite whetted for a couple of
years now for something more than an occasional
drink, an exchange of information, a few witty wise-
cracks. If she had chosen to give me more than a

cheerful time of day, I would have been in way over my head with that lady. For one of the few times in my adult life I had struck out swinging with a girl I really wanted. But I guess I was always ready to go to bat again.

She was giving me a kind of cat-in-the-cream smile as I fenced with the other press people. She knew perfectly well that, when the time came, she could pry anything out of me I had to give.

I was able to give Jody's competition enough to keep them happy for a while. Yes, Ted Valentine was the young man who had been linked with Sharon Brand for about a year. She'd been perfectly open about it, had even planned to discuss her older woman-younger man gig with Dick Thomas this afternoon. They knew about last night's scene in the Blue Lagoon. I told them the Medical Examiner placed the time of death at about then. I did not tell them that all Valentine's things had been missing from Sharon's suite. I couldn't tell them whether he'd been killed in the hotel, his body carried to the alley down the block, or whether he'd been killed in the alley. I didn't know.

"That's that," I told them.

"Miss Brand has had pretty bad luck with her young lovers." This from Eliot Stevens, a very solid reporter from one of the press associations.

I gave him my best public relations smile. "I guess I can tell you that's been duly noted, Eliot," I said. I didn't mention the further coincidence of the Dick Thomas Show. They would all have torn down the ballroom doors, where the show was due to go on in about an hour.

Jody was still giving me her dreamy smile. I wondered if she was reading my mind. But even before the circle around me broke up, I saw her drift away toward the staircase that leads up to the mezzanine and my office. Jody wasn't going to share the answers to any questions she might have with the rest of the press group. She knew I'd get to her just as quickly as I could.

I was supposed to be locating Chambrun, but I didn't see him anywhere in the crowded lobby. Neither Johnny Thacker, the day bell captain, nor Iverson on the front desk had seen him. I finally got to the house phone and had myself connected to Miss Ruysdale. She told me The Man was still "circulating." I explained that Sharon Brand wanted to see him and that I thought the lady was close to a new explosion point.

"I'll tell him as soon as he shows, Mark," Betsy Ruysdale said. "Have you tried the ballroom? He's got the Thomas Show on his mind, you know."

I made a decision then I was to regret later. "Will you try to get him on the phone there, Betsy? I've got an army of reporters to handle."

"Do my best," Betsy said.

My "army of reporters" consisted, at the moment, of one very attractive gal who was waiting for me in my office. My secretary had settled Jody into my private cubicle and provided her with coffee. Jody wasn't an infrequent visitor when she was on the trail of a story about one of our guests. I guess my secretary, a bright little thing, knew that I had seduction on my mind when Jody was in the offing.

"You're looking your lovely self," I said.

She was sitting in the leather chair next to my desk, her elegant legs crossed. I sensed that, unfortunately, she was all business this afternoon.

"You were skating around the outer edges of the ice down there, Mark," she said.

"You like a little slug of bourbon in that coffee?" I asked her. I sat down at my desk and produced a fifth of Jack Daniel's from my desk drawer.

"Much too early in the day for me," she said, "when I'm working. And stop undressing me, Mark."

I suppose I was looking at her that way. She knew, damn her, that I had one fixed intention about her. I think it amused her, but it sure as hell didn't move her. "What do you mean about the edges of the ice?" I asked her.

"You and Lieutenant Hardy and your Mr. Chambrun are surely aware that Victor Lewis disappeared on a day when Sharon Brand appeared on the Dick Thomas Show. Now this, on a day when she was due to appear again."

"How did you know that?"

"Stored away in my private computer," she said, and touched her forehead with the tip of a finger. "The Victor Lewis disappearance was a hot story for my purposes nearly three years ago."

"Two years and seven months," I said, and grinned at her.

"So you all know it's a coincidence you can't ignore," she said.

"It's not being ignored," I said.

"Some of the rest of the press boys and girls are going to wake up to it any minute," she said.

"So why didn't you ask about it down there?"

"In my business I'm always looking for any kind of edge on a story I can get," she said.

"So you know something that we know and that everyone else will wake up to any minute. It's not much of an edge, love."

"You might turn it into a solid edge for me, darling," she said. That was a meaningless "darling," just the way people in her world talk to each other.

I kept it light. "There's a price, of course."

Her dark eyes gave me a thoughtful look. "I know the price you have in mind, Mark. By now I think you know I'm a one-man-at-a-time woman. Paying your price would almost certainly be fun—but at the moment my flag is down."

"Who's driving the taxi?" I asked her.

"That is, quite simply, none of your business, Mark."

"So, how can I help you keep your edge?" There was no point in playing games with my dreams just now, it seemed.

She put down her empty coffee cup. "At the time Vic Lewis disappeared no one connected it in any way with the Dick Thomas Show. But I'm not a police reporter, Mark. Gossip is my business. Sharon Brand, the sex goddess, is prime meat for my grinder. I hate myself sometimes for prying into people's privacy, but that's how I make a living. It's what a huge public wants from me."

"I've never known you to be bitchy about anyone," I said.

"That doesn't mean I haven't had the ammunition," she said. "I'm thorough. No-stones-unturned department. I probably know more about Sharon Brand than she remembers about herself. I've got a file on her a foot thick."

"So?"

"So, I've made a study of Sharon Brand because she's always great copy. As a woman I was more than a little interested when she came out in the open with her older woman-younger man pronouncements."

"At your age a younger man would be too young to be any use to you," I said.

"I am thirty-one!" she said.

"My, my, what long teeth you have, grandma!"

"Ass!" she said. Then, with a kind of urgency, "We're using up time, Mark. I was interested in Sharon's life style. I wondered if Victor Lewis was a young opportunist taking advantage of a very rich, powerful-in-her-world, oversexed middle-aged broad. I did a track-down on Vic Lewis and he came up smelling like a rose. I convinced myself he was for real, that his relationship with Sharon was genuine, warm, serious. So when he disappeared, I never believed for a minute that he'd walked out on her. I didn't think of murder, Mark, until today, but I was certain there'd been some kind of violent accident, a drowning perhaps. He had a boat, sailed a lot. His boat, however, was where it should have been; his body never turned up. Police and Sharon's private eyes never came up with anything, but nothing could persuade me that he had just walked away and was hiding somewhere. I knew him, I'd interviewed him for a story, I was sure about him."

"Which brings us to—?" I asked.

"Which brings me to the Dick Thomas Show," Jody said. "Vic Lewis was trying to learn everything he could about Sharon's professional life. I don't suppose Red Baxter, Sharon's agent and manager, liked what he saw. Sharon is his main meal ticket, and he must have seen the handwriting on the wall. Sooner or later Vic Lewis would be given this particular plum by the lady herself. Baxter was too shrewd to scream and yell about it. Time might work for him. The young man might get tired of the older woman—he hoped. He didn't interfere with Vic's handling a small-potatoes thing like the Dick Thomas Show, a fifty-dollar commission. No harm in letting the boy get his feet wet in something so unimportant as a guest spot on Dick Thomas's hour and a half. So Vic Lewis set up that appearance on the Thomas Show in Hollywood. He spent time on it, mainly because Sharon was going to talk about her relationship with him. He helped Laura Sayles prepare the questions Dick Thomas would ask, making certain the interview would be in good taste. He was concerned about just how her entrance would be made, how she would be lighted, the works. He got to work with all the key people backstage. Then, when the time came, he wasn't there!''

"Not by choice," I said. "Something he couldn't help kept him away."

"For sure," Jody said. "I kept at it for a long time, Mark. Could he have gotten in someone's hair on the show? I even wondered about Red Baxter, the agent. Had he decided to make certain he didn't lose a million-dollar meal ticket?''

"Wow!" I said.

"Baxter, it turns out, has a long-term, unbreakable contract with Sharon," Jody said. "He didn't have to worry about Vic Lewis. I wrote him off. Then I concentrated on the Thomas people. There are about twenty-five regulars on the staff and crew, been with Thomas for years. I prepared a dossier on each one of them. It took months. Who had it in for Sharon Brand? Her career, her life, has touched thousands of people: other stars, supporting players, directors, lighting designers, cameramen, stagehands, gofors—the go-for-a-cup-of-coffee people. She could have stepped on someone, intentionally or unintentionally, rejected someone, cost someone a job, or—"

"She could have taken on almost anyone as a lover and then sent him packing," I said.

"The woods are full of those once-upon-a-times," Jody said.

"But why Vic Lewis? And now why, after nearly three years, Ted Valentine?"

"Who was, from what I gather, all the things you wondered about Vic Lewis—a greedy young opportunist taking advantage of an oversexed, middle-aged broad."

"But you have to think both these crimes were designed to hurt Sharon," Jody said.

"Hardy has her under police protection, if that gives you anything to add to your edge," I said.

"That isn't what you can do for me, Mark," Jody said. "I want to go backstage today, now, before the Thomas Show begins. I want to see who is there who was there two years and seven months ago. I want to see how some of them react to my being there again, snooping again, for the same reason—again. Some-one just might overreact."

"How do I help with that?"

She glanced at the little gold watch on her wrist. "It's almost time for them to let in the audience," she said. "They do a warm-up with the crowd when it's in. No one from the press is going to be allowed backstage once things begin. Too distracting for all the people who have specific jobs to do. But you could get me there, Mark. You're part of the scenery here at the

Beaumont. I suspect you can even walk through walls if you have to.''

"Or on water," I said. "Down through the kitchens and up the service elevators at the rear. It opens right into the backstage area.''

"You're an angel," she said. She was up out of her chair and I moved around from behind my desk to join her and lead the way. She stopped me with a hand on my shoulder. Then she tiptoed up and kissed me. For a fraction of a second I thought it was just a little warmer than a simple thank-you required. While there's life there's hope, I thought. I reached out for her, but she was headed "for the nearest exit."

THE SERVICE ELEVATOR from the kitchens is big enough to accommodate a small truck. When the ballroom is in normal use, long serving tables, loaded with buffet foods, can be wheeled on. On such occasions there was an operator to handle it, but that afternoon, not needed by the Thomas Show, it was on automatic. If the kitchen help or the engineer's people had seen strangers wandering around in the sub-levels, they would have been instantly stopped and questioned. I could go anywhere in the Beaumont, take anyone with me, and get no more than a smile and a wave of a hand.

The huge elevator lifted us up, noiselessly, to the ballroom level. Before the big gates opened to let us off, we could hear the waves of laughter and squeals of delight from the audience, occupying every one of the fifteen hundred seats available. Some stand-up comic was getting the crowd ready for Dick Thomas and his advertised guests, aided by Jake Floyd and the band, who improvised musical punctuation behind the jokes.

The set for the Thomas Show is a wide-open affair. Thomas's theory is that it fascinates the audience in the hall to see just how everything works—something the television screen doesn't show. The live audience can see the TV cameras moving in and out on dollies; the lighting people working from their control areas; the director and his assistants in a glassed-in control booth; the sound engineers at their place; the stagehands ready to move special props into place. Backstage, high above the center entrance, is a TV screen that monitors what is being seen by the television audience.

Backstage right is the bandstand where Jake Floyd and his boys work. Downstage left is a raised platform with half a dozen Windsor-type armchairs arranged along it in a line. Dick Thomas and his guests would occupy these for the interviews. The whole center area was reserved for the singers, dancers, and comics who would do their special numbers. Looking out at it from the wings, you were stunned by a vast technical operation—cameras, lights, microphones, miles of cables and cords. It looks so casual and informal when you see it on the screen, and so incredibly complicated when you see all that goes into it to make it happen.

Jody and I hadn't taken three steps off the service elevator when we were stopped by a dark, somewhat angry-looking young man wearing headphones and carrying a clipboard.

"Sorry, Miss Powers," he said. "We're about to roll. No visitors backstage."

"Hi, Pete," Jody said. "You know Mark Haskell, hotel P.R. This is Pete Banazak, Mark, the stage manager."

I recognized Banazak as a regular. He'd been in charge of the backstage the other times the Thomas

Show had come to the Beaumont. I'd never gotten to know him or talk to him. He'd always been too busy. He gave me a curt nod, but he obviously wasn't going to let us go any farther.

"I want to talk to you, Pete, and other friends I made on the staff and crew," Jody said.

"Sharon Brand's guy?" he asked.

She nodded.

"You have to know I can't let anyone be distracted during the show, Miss Powers," Banazak said. "You want to wait in the guest lounge until after the show, you may, but I can't have you talking to my people till we're off the air."

The guest lounge is an area set aside just off the stage area. It has comfortable chairs, a couch, a bar with drink makings and coffee, presided over by a Beaumont waiter. Here the day's guests can wait for their turn to appear. There is a TV monitor so the waiting performers can watch the show in progress.

I could see Jody wasn't happy when Banazak ushered us into the guest lounge. She wanted to circulate, to observe people. She was bitten by the crime-solving bug. I wanted to accommodate her for my own personal reasons, but with the show about to begin, I couldn't shoulder Banazak aside. He was going to be in charge for the next hour and a half or more.

I recognized the warm-up comic on the TV monitor. He was an old vaudevillian named Lenny Shields, who spends most of his working time these days playing the big hotels and night spots in Vegas. He was involved in a series of corny old mother-in-law jokes I'd cut my teeth on in sixth grade, but the audience seemed to think they were fresh and new and hilarious. I glanced at my watch and saw it was only about five minutes to air time. Lenny didn't have to hold the people for much longer.

Just then we were joined in the lounge by a good-looking young man wearing plaid slacks and pale pink summer jacket. He was Johnny Molloy, the Broadway musical comedy star. I knew him casually well. The Beaumont was a pet hangout of his. I remembered he was scheduled to be Dick Thomas's co-host for the week.

"Mark!" he said. "Long time no see."

He also knew Jody, embraced her, and gave her a show-business kiss on the cheek.

"I could dream I was going to be headlined in your column, my sweet," he said to her, "but I suspect you have a less happy reason for being here. Ghastly about Sharon Brand's young man." He looked at me. "Any new news?"

Johnny is a sort of new-generation Fred Astaire, a brilliant dancer, a pleasant singer, relaxed and charming. He was starring in the long-running musical *The Honey Man*, which was still selling out at the Winter Garden after a year and a half. Johnny was at the top of the heap in his world.

"Did you know Ted Valentine?" Jody asked him.

"Too well," Johnny said. "Practically not at all, which was too much in my book. You're only supposed to speak well of the dead, but he was a nasty piece in my book. It's a tough way to be rid of him, but I'd say Sharon is lucky."

Banazak stuck his head in the door. "Two minutes, Mr. Molloy," he said. "Watch the monitor, please."

"I'm co-hosting this opera for a week," Johnny said. "Slave labor."

"Tell me about Ted Valentine," Jody said.

"After the show, my sweet," he said, his eyes on the monitor.

Lenny Shields told his last joke to thunderous applause. The monitor went blank for a moment and we could hear the director's voice.

"Count down to air time. Nine—eight—seven— six—five—four—three—two—one—"

Jake Floyd's boys came in on cue with Dick Thomas's theme song. The announcer belted out his introduction.

"From the Hotel Beaumont in New York City—the Dick Thomas Show! And here, your host and mine, Dick Thomas!"

On the monitor Dick Thomas, blond and handsome, came through the center entrance. The applause mounted. Dick, bowing and smiling, carrying a hand mike, began to sing. He sings a popular tune about as well as anyone in the business. "I Get No Kick from Champagne—"

"The old bastard can really turn it on," Johnny said. "See you around, chums. For the next five minutes it's mine."

He left us. Dick Thomas finished his song and then, over the applause, he announced his first guest. "I'm fortunate this week to have as my co-host a great dancer, a great singer, star of *The Honey Man*, a great guy I'm proud to call my friend—Johnny Molloy!"

Johnny appeared on the screen, smiling his charming, crooked smile. He'd chosen an Old Fred Astaire favorite for his first number—"Top Hat, White Tie, and Tails." He began to dance, to mounting shouts, hand clappings, and girlish screams from the audience. He was a dream boat as he moved around the stage, singing as he danced.

"We're not going to get anywhere waiting here," Jody said.

"Look, I've got to catch up with Chambrun," I said. "Sit tight. If anything new has turned up, I'll come back and get you."

"I'll be somewhere around," she said. "Maybe I can think of some way to twist Pete Banazak's arm."

I grinned at her. "You know a way and so do I," I said.

"You're a sex freak," she said.

She touched my cheek with her cool fingers and I took off, wishing I didn't have to. Chambrun wasn't going to be pleased with me for having been out of touch for so long.

I didn't bother with the service elevator. I went down a back stair to the kitchen area and took one of the regular elevators up to the second floor. Betsy Ruysdale was in Chambrun's outer office, busy on the phone. She flagged me down as I headed for the The Man's inner sanctum, covered the phone mouthpiece with her hand.

"I have instructions for you. Hang on," she said.

A television set in the far corner was showing a picture but no sound. Johnny Molloy had finished his number and he and Dick Thomas were sitting together on the raised platform. The opening interview was in progress. The camera would shift to the audience from time to time, showing the customers laughing and delighted with whatever was going on.

Ruysdale finished her phone call and gave her attention to me. "The boss has gone up to Fourteen to see Miss Brand," she said. "He's been trying to reach Red Baxter, her agent and manager, in Hollywood. Endless busy signals. I suppose half the movie world is after Baxter to find out what he knows about what's happened. I'm flooded with calls here. The boss wants you to keep after Baxter till you reach him.''

"To tell him what?"

"To tell him to hold on while you switch him through to Mr. Chambrun."

I went into The Man's office to try to carry out his orders. Ruysdale had supplied me with Baxter's numbers, office and home. It was nearly five o'clock here, two o'clock out there. Both numbers were busy. I finally got through to a chief operator, told her it was a police emergency and to cut through any calls to Baxter's office.

I didn't get Baxter, but a harried-sounding secretary. It took her a moment or two to realize who I was and why I was calling.

"Mr. Baxter is on his way to the airport," she told me. "American Airlines, Flight 307. It is due in New York about one A.M. your time. He'll be going to the Beaumont to be with Miss Brand, of course."

I called Fourteen B and gave Chambrun the news. I couldn't tell what his reaction was to it. If he'd had Jody's notion that Red Baxter might be involved in the Valentine violence, this seemed to clear him.

"Anything special you want me to do?" I asked him.

"Ear to the ground," he said.

I told him about Jody Powers and her theories and that she was backstage at the Thomas Show, attempting to check out on staff and crew.

"Smart girl," Chambrun said. "I know it won't cause you any pain to stick with her. If she stumbles on anything, let me know."

I took an elevator down to the basement area and walked into bedlam. People were crowded around the open gates to the service elevators, which were open except the car wasn't there. People from the kitchen in white work clothes, maintenance people in jeans and work shirts, all talking at once.

Scotty McPherson, the chief engineer on the day shift, stopped me as I moved forward to see what it was all about.

"Messy business, Mr. Haskell," he said. "Woman fell down the service elevator shaft from quite high up, I imagine. Smashed to pieces."

"Where's the car?" I asked.

"Stopped up at Eleven," he said. "The woman must have fallen from Ten, or Nine, just below the car."

"Gates don't open if the car isn't there, do they?" I asked.

"Unless you know how," McPherson said.

I pushed forward and looked into the grease-filled bottom of the shaft. I couldn't believe what I saw. There was no mistaking that summer print dress, the dark hair matted with blood, the little gold wristwatch on a shattered arm. Beyond any doubt or hope it was Jody Powers.

I turned away in a hurry. I thought I was going to vomit.

PART TWO

ONE

No MORE THAN four or five minutes ago Jody had been alive. At least it was only that long ago that her body had come hurtling down the elevator shaft to the pit, the end of the line. It was only forty minutes ago, not more, that I'd left her waiting in the guest lounge backstage, just one floor up. In those spans of time a lovely, vital, intelligent human being had been snuffed out. She had been looking, I thought, for a murderer, and, God help her, she had found him!

Jerry Dodd, our security chief, came charging down the corridor from the main elevators. McPherson had called for him, managed to keep others from making the futile effort to help Jody. She was too dead to need help.

Jerry saw me standing to one side, and my face must have been pale green from the nausea that had swept over me. He stopped, guessing what had hit me.

"Someone you know, Mark?"

"Jody Powers," I said in a voice I didn't recognize as my own.

"Good Christ!" he said. He knew Jody. She had spent so much time in the Beaumont, talking to her precious celebrities. I think he knew she meant more to me than just a guest I was polite to as part of my job. He probably thought she was more to me than she ever had been. Not because I hadn't wanted more and tried to get it. It wasn't just a physical encounter I'd been trying for. I had wanted to share her wit, her intelligence, her affection, her love—if she could have found love for me. She had been so special, so very special. *Had been!* I almost choked on that.

"She was backstage in the ballroom," I told Jerry. "I left her there half an hour, forty minutes ago. I was on my way back to join her when—" I waved vaguely toward the crowd around the elevator shaft.

Jerry didn't ask me what Jody was doing backstage at the Dick Thomas Show. Being around stars and celebrities had been her business. *Had been!*

I stood leaning against a stone pillar, unable to follow Jerry to where it was at. I heard him ask McPherson where the service car was. I suppose McPherson pointed to the indicator above the gates.

"Eleven," the engineer said.

"Don't let anybody bring it down till we've looked at it," Jerry said.

"I've already shut off the power," McPherson said.

"She was just one flight up in the ballroom," Jerry said.

"She didn't fall from there," McPherson said. "That's not more than twenty feet. She could have been hurt bad, maybe even killed from such a fall. But what's in there, Mr. Dodd, is hamburger. She fell from high up."

"The gates are closed except when the car is at a floor," Jerry said. "There's no way to open a gate by accident and fall down the shaft."

"No way—by accident," McPherson said.

I knew damn well that what had happened to Jody was no kind of an accident. Someone had gotten her into that service car by force, or some other way, carried her up to say the tenth floor, forced her out, sent the car up to Eleven with its automatic controls. Then he had gotten the gates at Ten open, knowing how, and sent her, probably screaming, down the black hole to her death. That someone had to have started with her from the ballroom, from the Dick Thomas Show, from the guest lounge.

I don't know if I can explain to you what happened to me about then. The nausea had passed me by, and what I felt was a churning rage that had my heart pounding against my ribs, my temples throbbing, my muscles tensed. What I was going to do was as simple as ABC. I was going up to the ballroom and kill somebody! Just as simple and uncomplicated as that.

I should have notified Chambrun of what had happened. McPherson had probably already done that. Routine, when anything out of the ordinary happened. I should have told Jerry Dodd what Jody had been doing backstage at the Thomas Show. It would take too long. The Thomas Show was still on the air, about ten or twelve minutes to go. The man I was to kill was back on the job, unless he'd taken a powder, which would have been like a confession.

I headed for the stairway to the ballroom. Nobody tried to stop me. They were all too concerned with the "hamburger" at the bottom of the shaft.

When I reached the backstage area, Buddy Sellers was singing that crazy song of his.

Mamma, I gotta tell you it hurts.
Mamma, I gotta tell you it hurts.
Mamma, I gotta tell you it hurts.
It hurts, it hurts, it hurts—

And then Banazak, the stage manager, was standing in front of me.

"Here again, Mr. Haskell?" he said. "I have to remind you, you can't wander around backstage. One of the cameras will pick you up by mistake. We have about ten minutes to go. The guest lounge—"

I grabbed him by his shirt front. "You listen to me, you sonofabitch, and listen good," I said. "You know everything that goes on back here during the show. See all, know all. That's you, Buster."

He tried to wrench free, but I had hold of him for keeps. "What the hell's the matter with you?" he said, obviously startled. "And keep your voice down! You want to broadcast to the whole effing United States?"

"Where is Jody Powers?" I asked him.

"In the guest lounge where you left her, I suppose," he said.

"You've been bringing guests on and off out of that lounge for the last hour," I said. "You know damn well she isn't there."

"I tell you—"

"I'll tell you what you tell me," I said. "Somebody took Jody out of that guest lounge to the service elevator. You saw it. You see everything, you know everything."

"I watch the show. I'm only concerned with the mechanics of the show," he said. He looked at me as if he thought I was off my rocker. Maybe I was.

"Let me tell you, Buster, how it is," I said. "Someone from this set, this show, took Jody to the service elevator, carried her up eight or ten floors, and shoved her down the shaft. She fell to the basement. She's dead, murdered. So who was it? You must have seen. You see everything."

I let go of his shirt and took a step back. I was going to let him have one right in the mouth if he didn't talk.

Mamma, I gotta tell you it hurts.
Mamma, I gotta tell you it hurts—

The audience was clapping and stomping to the crazy rhythm. Banazak's eyes were wide as saucers. The tip of his tongue appeared and moistened his lips.

"I don't believe it!" he said in something like a whisper.

"Believe," I said. "And talk, because if you don't—"

A heavy hand fell on my shoulder. I spun around, ready to take on the world. It was Lieutenant Hardy.

"Easy, son," he said. His fingers were like grappling hooks in my shoulder. He looked past me to Banazak. "I'm Lieutenant Hardy of Homicide. You're the stage manager?"

Banazak nodded. Sweat was running down his face.

"Spread the word as fast as you can," Hardy said. "No guests, no members of the staff or crew, are to leave this area when the show is over. I have all the exits covered. Anyone who tries to leave will be arrested."

Banazak streaked off. Buddy Sellers was reaching his climax.

It hurts, it hurts, it hurts—

Would you believe I buried my face against Hardy's broad chest and burst into tears? My hero moment was passed.

LOOKING BACK on that whole day, I have the sensation of being caught in the center of a whirlpool of people. First there had been the crazy yammering in the lobby of the people who wanted to get into the Dick Thomas Show. Now, the show over, there was a swirling of the people who'd been on it and run it. There were cops at a half dozen exit doors, the staff and crew milling around in shirt sleeves and street clothes, Dick Thomas and his guests, wearing makeup for the cameras, looking like confused and displaced circus clowns.

Minutes ago only one person, a killer, had known what had happened. The minute Dick Thomas signed off on camera it was as if someone had set off an explosion. Sky writing! Within seconds thirty-five or forty people had the word, the news.

Standing in the center of the stage, an actor in a lighted area, was Hardy. From the control booth, over a loudspeaker, came the voice of Tony Meador, the show's director.

"Quiet, please, everyone."

The babel of voices was instantly hushed.

"The police believe a murder has been committed backstage during the course of the show. That is why you are being asked to stay here. In centerstage is Lieutenant Hardy of Manhattan Homicide. Pay attention to him."

Some young man, a member of the crew, hurried up to Hardy with a hand mike. He took it, looking at it as though it might be a bomb. He cleared his throat and it sounded like coal going down a chute. He wasn't used to mikes.

"The unfortunate victim of a murderous attack is Jody Powers, the well-known columnist," he said. There was a swelling of incredulous voices and then complete silence again. "Miss Powers was visiting backstage," Hardy went on. "She was in the guest

lounge for at least a while, accompanied by Mark
Haskell, the public relations man for the hotel." Suddenly everyone was looking at me. "Mr. Haskell left
her there to attend to other business in the hotel.
Sometime after that, while the show was in progress,
Miss Powers was persuaded or forced to go with
someone to the service elevator. She was taken up ten
or eleven floors in that elevator and then thrown down
the shaft to her death." Again the swell of voices, and
then silence. "It is not impossible that the killer is here
on this stage. It is not at all unlikely that someone,
paying no particular attention, saw Miss Powers leave
the guest lounge with someone and head for the service elevator." Hardy looked around at the tense faces,
waiting for someone to speak. No one did.

"So we have to go about it another way," Hardy
said. "At what point during the show did it happen?
We know that Miss Powers' body came down the shaft
about fifteen minutes before the show ended. When she
was taken away is something else again. How many of
you here knew that Miss Powers was backstage?"

Johnny Molloy, the dancer, the co-host, was the first
one to raise his hand. He had been wiping makeup off
his face with a stained Kleenex.

"I'm John Molloy, Lieutenant," he said. "I co-
hosted the show with Dick. I went into the guest lounge
three or four minutes before the show began. Miss
Powers was there with Mark—Mark Haskell. She was
an old friend. We said hello, passed the time of day.
Then I got my cue to go on and I left them. From then
on, Lieutenant, I was onstage, performing, taking part
as co-host in the interviews. I was never out of sight of
Dick Thomas, the cameras, the director, the stage
managers. I was not, could not have been, your man."

Banazak's hand was up. "I'm Pete Banazak, the stage manager," he said. "I first saw Miss Powers when she appeared backstage with Haskell before the show started. This seems to be your day for violence, Lieutenant. I asked Miss Powers and she told me she'd come to question people on the show about the murder of Ted Valentine. I told her—and Haskell—they'd have to wait till after the show, and I directed them to the guest lounge. That's the last I saw of them until Haskell reappeared backstage just before the show ended. He told me the shocking news."

"You didn't see Miss Powers again after you first directed her to the guest lounge?" Hardy asked.

"No, sir."

"But you direct all the backstage traffic, Mr. Banazak. If Miss Powers was wandering around outside that guest lounge with someone, wouldn't you have been likely to notice?"

"Yes—but I didn't."

Two other young men, assistant stage managers, stepped forward. They had known, before the show started, that Jody was backstage. One of them, whose name turned out to be Buzz Picone, hadn't seen her, but he had been told by Banazak that she was in the guest lounge and ordered to make certain she didn't start wandering around, talking to people.

"So you were watching the guest lounge all through the show?" Hardy asked.

"Hell no, Lieutenant," Picone said. "I have my special duties on the show. I took a look back in that direction from time to time, but I couldn't say I was watching all the time. I had a job to do."

"So she could have left the guest lounge and you wouldn't have seen her?"

"Sure. You can leave the guest lounge without being seen in the stage area. Rear door opens to the dressing rooms, the johns." Picone moistened his lips. "The service elevator is just behind it."

He was right about that, I realized. You could leave the guest lounge through that rear door and no one working in the stage area could see you. It was set up that way on purpose. A guest on the show could go from his dressing room to the lounge without any chance of being picked up by a roving camera. The lounge was a sort of way station, where the guests waited for their cue to go on. But the guests were cued on by the stage manager or one of his assistants. That meant that every six or seven minutes Banazak, or Picone, or this other guy, whose name turned out to be Wally Brown, stuck his head in the door to the stage side of the lounge to warn the guest that he was about to be on. That meant that every six or seven minutes during the hour and a half of the show a stage manager, cueing on a guest, would know whether Jody was still in the lounge.

It turned out that on this afternoon Wally Brown had been assigned to cueing on the guests. I remembered now he'd come to the door to cue on Johnny Molloy while I was there. Hardy had worked this out for himself and he worked on Brown, patiently tough.

"So you saw Miss Powers in the lounge, Brown?"

"Oh, sure," Brown said. He wasn't enjoying the heat, and he kept wiping his mouth with the back of his hand. "I went to cue on Johnny Molloy and she was there with Mr. Haskell."

"After that," Hardy said.

"How do you mean?"

"When did you see her again?"

Brown had a clipboard tucked under his arm. He took it out and looked at it. "Ross Lubelle was next," he said. "She was there when I cued Mr. Lubelle on."

Ross Lubelle, the actor, is a dark, romantically sinister-looking young man who was playing the current version of the *Dracula* syndrome on Broadway. Theater audiences are apparently mad for plays about the blood-sucking count from Transylvania. He stepped forward, wearing a handsomely tailored blue tropical worsted suit.

"I can vouch for that, Lieutenant. I'm Ross Lubelle," he said. "Jody was in the lounge when I went into it from my dressing room. We were old friends. My God, Lieutenant, that this should have happened to her!"

"You talked with her?" Hardy asked.

Lubelle nodded. I thought he seemed shaken. "We talked about Sharon Brand's unfortunate young man."

"You talked about murder?"

"Yes. Never dreaming, of course, that—that—" Lubelle couldn't go on.

"Thank you, Mr. Lubelle," Hardy said. He turned back to young Brown, who was studying his clipboard. "When did you next see Miss Powers, Brown?"

Brown pointed to his board. "Sally Cleaves, the nightclub singer, was next. When I cued her on, Miss Powers was still in the lounge."

Hardy looked out at the faces surrounding him. A handsome young black woman raised her hand. "I'm Sally Cleaves, Lieutenant. Miss Powers *was* there when I went into the lounge. I didn't know her, but when we exchanged names I knew who she was, of course. We chatted for a moment about the show and how it was going, and then Wally cued me on."

"Thank you, Miss Cleaves. The next time you saw her, Brown?"

Brown was scowling at his list. "The doctor fellow was next." He studied his list. "Dr. Snodgrass. He's written a book on child abuse. Dick interviewed him."

"Was Miss Powers there when you cued the doctor on?"

"I—I honestly don't remember. The doctor wasn't show business. He'd had no rehearsal. I had to seeing-eye-dog him out to place him in the wings, keep him from tripping over cables. I just don't remember if Miss Powers was there. I mean, I wasn't concerned about her."

A tall, bony man with thick shell-rimmed glasses stepped forward. "Perhaps I can help you, Lieutenant," he said. "I'm Dr. Ralph Snodgrass. I can tell you that there was no one in the lounge when I was directed there from the dressing rooms."

"You're positive?"

"Of course I'm positive. No one was there."

Dick Thomas had kept a low profile during the questioning. He'd been involved in a whispered conversation with Lou Feldman, his producer. This was going to raise hell with his show for the rest of the week, perhaps even longer. If anyone on his staff or any of his guests had done for Jody, the going for him would be rough, the press hurrah damaging. But he spoke now.

"I think Wally can tell you exactly what time it was Dr. Snodgrass was cued on, Lieutenant. We keep a time chart on the show in progress, so that we always know if we're behind or if we have to stretch it out."

Wally Brown looked at his clipboard. "Five twenty-four," he said.

So Jody had been gone from the lounge then, a little less than an hour before she'd plunged down the
shaft. Where had she gone? Who had she talked with?
Most important of all, who had been missing from his
post on the show after 5:24?

Answering those questions involved the kind of
dogged drudgery at which Hardy was expert. It drove
me up the wall. I needed action!

TWO

I SHOULD HAVE KNOWN where I'd find it the minute Hardy gave me permission to leave. It was going to take him endless time to check and cross-check with all those people gathered on the ballroom stage. He was running into an occupational headache. Everybody on the Dick Thomas Show, the staff and crew, had an "urgent appointment" they were already late for. Hardy wasn't a man to be rushed or flustered. He let me go, because the critical time for Jody had come after I'd left her to go look for Chambrun and before I'd headed back to catch up with her again. He let Johnny Malloy go. Johnny really did have an urgent appointment. He was due in his dressing room at the Winter Garden to ready himself for that night's performance of *The Honey Man*. Furthermore he'd been on stage, on camera, the entire length of the show. People had seen Jody long after he'd made his initial entrance.

Dick Thomas was equally well alibied, in view of cameras and audience the whole time, but his close connection with all the people involved kept him Hardy's prisoner. Nor did he ask to leave. These were "his people."

With some reluctance I went back down the stairway to the basement. Mercifully, the Medical Examiner's crew had removed what was left of Jody from the bottom of the service shaft. Plainclothes cops were keeping people away from the place where Jody had died. A couple of Scotty McPherson's boys were sifting through the grease and dirt for the police, searching for whatever. I guessed they hoped to find something that might tie in the killer—a button off his coat, a piece of cloth, anything.

Jerry Dodd was gone. McPherson told me he was up on Eleven with more cops, fingerprinting the service car. The killer had to have fingered the control buttons, the gate he'd gotten open so that Jody, dead or alive at the time, could be sent tumbling down the shaft. There had to be a lead somewhere, some minuscule trace of the bastard I had every intention of removing from the scene, permanently. I was still dreaming that dream.

The lobby was almost back to normal, unless you knew the climate as well as I did. The mob of Dick Thomas fans was gone, unaware that a murder had been committed while they sat there laughing, clapping, giving out the girlish shrieks of delight. But there were still armies of people from the press, newspapers, television, radio. They had two murders to claw at and, so far, nobody had given them anything to write about or talk about except the bare facts that Ted Valentine had been clubbed to death in an alley down the block and that Jody Powers, one of their own, had fallen or been pushed down an elevator shaft. Hardy had made himself unavailable. Chambrun, always good copy, couldn't be reached. Miss Ruysdale had built a stone wall around him. I was a gleam of light to them when I walked out into the open, and they swarmed around me like a pack of hungry wild dogs.

"I don't have anything to tell you," I told them. "I don't know anything—except that the police don't believe Jody's death was an accident."

"How? Who? What? Where? When?"

I looked around at them and realized that I was damn near dead on my feet from physical and emotional exhaustion. I held up my hand for silence.

"I'll do the best I can for you," I said. "I'll set up a room for the press just off the lobby, there, next to the Spartan Bar. When Hardy's ready to make a statement, I'll have him come to you there. When I have anything I'm free to tell you, I'll tell you. Mike Maggio, the night bell captain, will see to it you can get food, coffee, booze, whatever you want."

"We want facts, Mark," Eliot Stevens said. "The Beaumont seems to have been turned into a slaughterhouse. That kind of background color isn't going to do you any good, you know."

I was half blinded by a flashbulb. Some jerk photographer was going to have me on the front page of a morning newspaper. Eliot Stevens from International is a good, honest newsman and I tried to give him a good, honest answer.

"The hotel is open to the public, Eliot," I told him. "There's no way on earth we can prepare in advance against some kind of psychotic killer. What's happened here could happen in Times Square, or in the Plaza, or the Waldorf. The Beaumont can't be blamed."

"Jody Powers was working on the Valentine case," Eliot said. "Did she uncover something? If she did, that would mean Valentine's murderer is still circulating here, under your roof."

"Let me say, I think the thought has occurred to Lieutenant Hardy," I said. "Now, let me set up a room for you, and when there's anything solid to tell you, I'll tell you."

I left them, went to the desk, beckoning to Mike Maggio on the way. I arranged with Mr. Atterbury at the desk and Mike to set up what is called the Carnation Room for the reporters. Then I took a quick powder up to the second floor.

One of Jerry Dodd's security men and Maggie Malone, Miss Ruysdale's secretary—the secretary's secretary—were in Chambrun's outer office.

"They're both inside," Maggie told me.

Chambrun was at his desk, with Betsy Ruysdale standing behind him. He was just putting down the phone as I walked in. He looked at me and I saw that rare look of compassion in his deep-set eyes.

"I'm very sorry for you, Mark," he said. "I know you were fond of the Powers girl."

Sympathy from The Man, in my condition, was almost too much. I felt myself teetering on the verge of childish tears again.

"Unfortunately," he said, his voice gone flat, "we still have a hotel to run under the most difficult conditions. We cannot afford the luxury of anger."

"Anger?" I asked, walking right into his Sunday punch.

"It's written all over you," he said. "Heroic knight on a white charger, who also plays the roles of judge and executioner. That kind of nonsense tends to blur your vision and dull your effectiveness. Be good enough to remember, Mark, that you are an employee of this hotel, not the romantic lead in *Superman-Two*."

"Then fire me!" I said, forgetting about self-pity. "Jody was my friend."

"Then serve her in the best way you can," Chambrun said, almost as though he was bored with the conversation. "Use your expertise about this hotel, your knowledge of how to handle the public and the press, to assist the people whose job it is to bring criminals to justice.''

"Meaning you and Hardy?" I asked, my feathers ruffled.

"And the District Attorney's office, and the Medical Examiner's office, and the Los Angeles police if they're brought into the case. Have you forgotten, Mark, that your Miss Powers is just a minor distraction in a pattern of a major crime?"

"A minor distraction? For God sake, boss, how can you—"

"We started out to hunt for a man bent on killing Sharon Brand's young lovers," Chambrun said. "Miss Powers simply got in someone's way. If she hadn't tried to do the same thing you have in mind, amateur meddling, she would probably be here now, helping us with her own special expertise."

"Which was what?"

"The professional invasion of other people's privacy," he said. The tone of his voice indicated how low his opinion was of gossip as a business. "What did she think she knew, Mark? Why did she need you to get her backstage at the Thomas Show?"

"Just a hunch, I think."

I told him that Jody had arrived at the same conclusion that he had, which ought to be a plus for her. She thought there was a connection between the disappearance of Victor Lewis and the murder of Ted Valentine. She didn't think it was a coincidence that both events had taken place when Sharon Brand was on, or due to be on, the Dick Thomas Show. She had checked out all the people on Thomas's staff and crew when

Lewis disappeared. She wanted to find out who was still involved with the show this second time.

"She named no names?" Chambrun asked.

"No. She did say she had a file 'a foot thick' on Sharon Brand. She probably has files on some of Thomas's people."

"Where would she keep those files?"

"In her apartment, I suppose. She didn't have an office. A duplex in the East Seventies. She has a girl who is a combination secretary and researcher. Nancy Armin, her name is."

"Call her," Chambrun said. "Warn her that someone may be after those files. Go see her and take a look at those files if she'll show them to you. It'll do you good to get out of the hotel. I'll arrange with Hardy to have that apartment watched."

"But—"

"Move," Chambrun said.

I WAS DISMISSED. The Man is a pretty wise kind of a guy, though. I needed something to do, and he'd provided me with it, away from the slow-moving police investigation and the scene of a horror I wasn't going to be able to shake for a long time.

I tried to call Nancy Armin at Jody's apartment. The line seemed to be perpetually busy, but I finally got through. Nancy was in shock. The ladies and gentlemen of the press had provided her with the news long before it was carried on radio or TV. Nancy is a nice girl, a couple of years out of Vassar, with long legs and nearsighted blue eyes. Vanity kept her from wearing glasses except when she had to read something. She leaned toward you when you talked to her as if she was

intensely interested. It was flattering until you realized
that she was just trying to see you clearly.

She sounded relieved to hear from me. I was a friend
of Jody's, the only friend who had, so far, called. I told
her not to let anyone in till I got there. She promised.

It was only ten blocks away from the Beaumont, but
I took a taxi. Nancy opened the door of Jody's fif-
teenth-floor duplex in a plush apartment building almost before I got my finger off the doorbell. She didn't
ask who it was.

"I could have been Jack the Ripper," I told her.

She just collapsed into my arms, shaking and trembling, fighting tears. "It is so awful, so senseless, so—
so ghastly!" she managed to say.

I ferried her into the apartment, closing and chain-
bolting the door behind us. I knew the attractive living
room well, with its paintings by some French impres-
sionists. Jody had loved bright colors, and the curtains, the upholstery, the rugs, reflected that love.

We spent a little time, sitting together on the couch,
her fingers locked in mine like a vise, while I told her
about the last hour or so of Jody's life, a time I'd spent
with her. That brought me around to the files.

"They're not going to be much use to you, Mark—
or anyone else," she said.

"Why not? She spent her life gathering information
about people." I didn't use Chambrun's phrase about
"the professional invasion of other people's privacy."

"Jody—" It hurt this girl even to mention Jody's
name. "Jody wasn't your everyday scandalmonger,"
Nancy said. "She wrote interesting things about interesting people. They confided in her because they
trusted her. Scandalous stories did come her way, of
course. People tried to curry her favor by passing on

dirt about other people. Other people tried to sell her dirt. There's no way she could avoid hearing it all, knowing about it all. But it's not in the files, Mark.''

"But surely she needed to know, if someone—''

"She talked about it to me quite often,'' Nancy said. "There were aspects of her business she didn't like. She always said she could be the greatest blackmailer on earth if she chose. But there's not one item of dirt in the files, there isn't a dossier on anyone she wouldn't quite happily show to the person it was about.''

"Where did she keep the dirt?'' I asked.

"In her computer,'' Nancy said, and gave me a teary smile.

"What computer?''

"Her head,'' Nancy said. I suddenly remembered Jody tapping her forehead with a slender finger and referring to her "computer.'' "Nobody could find anything in the files that they couldn't find out for themselves with a little effort.''

"She said she had a file a foot thick on Sharon Brand.''

"A thirty-year career, Mark. What's there is a date of birth—which Sharon might not care to have revealed; place of birth, name of parents, marriage or marriages, children if any, the titles of all the pictures in which she's played and the names of the actors who played with her, awards, probably hundreds of photographs, professional and casual. It's all there for a biographer who might be interested. But the dirt is gone.''

"Gone where?''

Nancy began to shake again. "Down that elevator shaft,'' she said in a choked voice. "There must have been endless scandalous facts and rumors about Sharon Brand."

"And about others, people involved with Dick Thomas?"

"Gone, Mark. They were never put on paper and so they're gone. I don't need a policeman to protect me or the files. There's nothing for anyone to steal that they couldn't find out for themselves with a little effort. Anything that could hurt anyone is gone."

"But does anyone know that but you—and now me?" I asked her.

I had never seen the upper floor of Jody's duplex, though goodness knows I'd tried hard enough to make it. Her bedroom, dressing room, and bath were there. There was also a second bedroom and bath which Nancy Armin used on those days or nights that Jody was working around the clock. The rest of the upper floor was one huge studio room—two rooms had been knocked together—barely furnished: two desks, two typewriters, and the wall on three sides consisting of metal filing cabinets. The fourth wall was a built-in bookcase, crowded to overflowing. It was strictly a place for working.

Several manila filing folders were lying on the top of Jody's typewriter.

"Just the way she left them when the news broke about Ted Valentine," Nancy told me. "She took off in high gear for the Beaumont when she heard."

I glanced idly at the folders. One was labeled *Ted Valentine*; one—and it was damn near a foot thick— labeled *Sharon Brand*; one labeled *Claudine Trudeau*. That last one didn't ring any bells for me. I flipped it open and glanced at the single typewritten sheet it contained.

Claudine Trudeau: Born Paris, France, 1951. Parents: Claude and Suzanne Trudeau. Family emigrated to New York when Claudine was four. No address for parents.

Alongside this typed paragraph Jody had written in her bold handwriting: "This information from Universal. I don't believe a word of it. Claudine was no more French than my Aunt Sally."

The typescript went on: "Apprentice in summer stock in 1970, Sharon, Connecticut. Rex Hilliard was starring there in a new play—*The Game Plan*. When that run was over, Hilliard took Claudine out to Hollywood, where she got a contract with Universal. Appeared in a quickie B picture—*The Boys on the Beach*. Acting talent consisted mostly of looking sexy in a bikini. No other film. Some extra bits in TV, according to the studio.

"Suicide—by drowning—1974."

Again Jody's handwriting. "Right out of *A Star Is Born*. She left a note and just walked out into the ocean. Body recovered by the Coast Guard some days later."

I showed the typewritten page to Nancy. "You know what was interesting about this?"

She had to go over to her desk for glasses. "It's not one I've seen before. You understand, Mark, there are hundreds and hundreds of names with some kind of comment on them. If I'd stopped to look at them all, I'd never have gotten my work done. I draw a blank on Claudine Trudeau." She frowned. When she frowned, her nose wrinkled up. She was a cute girl. "I seem to remember that Rex Hilliard made several films with Sharon Brand— In a thick file like hers there is a sort

of cross-index in front. I know because I made most of
them for Jody.''

There were literally hundreds of names on Sharon's
index pages. Rex Hilliard's was there. I referred to the
page in the file where he was listed. He had made four
films with Sharon. There was a casual photograph of
them together, wearing parkas and snow boots. The
date on it was 1973.

Sharon Brand and Rex Hilliard on location in
Aspen, Colorado, where they were shooting a new
film tentatively titled *Downhill Is the Way to the
Top*.

"It was a big hit, as I remember," Nancy said. "I
saw it when—when I was quite a bit younger."

There was no indexing of Claudine Trudeau in the
Brand file.

I glanced at the Ted Valentine file. It was skimpy.
He'd been born in 1955. Parents, George and Martha,
retired to Florida. Camera technician. Not with any
one job very long. No one had paid very much attention to him till 1978. There was a picture to explain
that. It showed Valentine waving at a photographer.
The caption—I suspected this had been published in
the *Star* or some other scandal sheet—read: "Sharon
Brand's new young man." That had earned him a place
in Jody's files.

There was a reference to Claudine Trudeau in Valentine's file. I thought Jody might have had the Trudeau file out when she got the word about Valentine's
murder, for some reason or other. When someone
phoned her about Valentine, she'd gotten out his file

and Sharon's without bothering to put the Trudeau file back in the cabinet where it belonged.

Still it nagged at me. "Is there a file on Rex Hilliard?" I asked Nancy. "He knew this Trudeau dame from summer stock, sounds like he got her a contract at Universal."

Nancy went over to the file cabinets and brought me back a folder on Rex Hilliard. It was fairly extensive, with a couple of studio photographs of the actor, one as a young juvenile, one quite recent. He had aged into his fifties gracefully. He had appeared with all the great stars of the last quarter century. He had been married to four famous ladies. There was a mention of that stock performance in 1970, but nothing about Claudine Trudeau. She didn't appear anywhere in his file.

Claudine Trudeau, whoever she was, kept getting in the way of more urgent things. Was there a file on Dick Thomas? Two years and seven months ago Jody Powers had had a hunch that there was some connection between the Thomas operation and the disappearance of Vic Lewis. A file on the Thomas Show might tell us what had made Jody so dangerous to someone.

Nancy produced the file for me and it was almost as thick as the one on Sharon Brand. After all, Dick Thomas had been doing his show for something like twenty years. He must have provided a lot of copy for Jody during the five or six years she'd been doing her column.

I saw at once that the Thomas file was going to be interesting to Hardy and his Homicide boys. There were notes on twenty or twenty-five people in addition to Thomas: Lou Feldman, the producer; Laura Sayles, the Twiggy-type researcher; Tony Meador, the director; Pete Banazak, the stage manager; and his assistants Buzz Picone and Wally Brown; others to whom I couldn't put faces. Jody was going to save the cops an awful lot of digging. It was all here, spelled out, person by person. Or was it? How much had been stored away in Jody's "computer," which would never be revealed?

I called Chambrun and told him what I'd found. He sounded pleased, and said he would get word to Hardy at once. The Thomas file could shorten and sharpen the Lieutenant's interrogation of the people who were being held in the ballroom.

I had one more rather intimate question to ask Nancy. Just a little while ago Jody had turned me off with her little speech about being a one-man-at-a-time girl. Somewhere there was a guy who would be flattened when he heard the news.

"Who was Jody's man-of-the-moment?" I asked Nancy. "Does he know what's happened?"

Nancy gave me a kind of blank stare.

"I know there is a guy, Nancy. Jody told me, only today."

"I tried to reach him," she said. "He's a pilot. His name is Ben Stryker—Captain Ben Stryker. He flies an overseas run for TWA—London, Paris, Cairo. I called Crew Schedule at TWA to find out where he is. He's off."

"Off where?"

"That's the problem, Mark. They take a three or four day trip, and then they get three or four days off, maybe more. Ben—Captain Stryker—is in between flights and I have no idea where to find him. He doesn't answer the phone at his apartment. Crew Schedule doesn't know where he is. No reason they should. He isn't supposed to check in for a couple of days. He could be anywhere."

"He didn't spend his free time with Jody?"

"Most always. But now and then, when he was off and Jody was facing some sort of deadline, he'd go somewhere. He's a golf nut. He likes to play courses all over the place. He could be in a tournament somewhere, but goodness knows where."

"Jody would have known where, wouldn't she?"

"Of course, but she wouldn't necessarily tell me. Ben—Captain Stryker—will probably call sometime this evening. He usually calls every night when he's away somewhere. He—he's very much in love with Jody."

Nancy and I were on our way downstairs when the front doorbell sounded. I checked through the peephole and saw an obvious cop in plainclothes who held out his shield for me to see. He clearly had no connection with the call I'd just made to Chambrun. This one had been ordered earlier to come here to protect Nancy and Jody Powers's files.

"Oh, I'll stay," she said. "There'll be endless phone calls from friends, business associates, as soon as the news is really out. Ben—Captain Stryker—will almost certainly call from wherever he is, whether he's heard the news or not. I wouldn't want him to find himself talking to a policeman—if he hasn't heard."

I thought I saw a faint surge of color in Nancy's cheeks. The way she stumbled around the name— "Ben—Captain Stryker—" I got the notion Jody's boyfriend meant just a little more to Miss Nancy than she wanted me to know.

THREE

THERE IS AN OLD JOKE I heard some vaudeville comic tell when I was a kid. A drunk walks up to a policeman on the beat and says, "Officer, would you be good enough to tell me where I am?" The cop says, "You're at the corner of Broadway and Forty-second Street." The drunk says, "Never mind the detail. What town am I in?"

It was about nine in the evening when I reported back to Chambrun at the Beaumont. The only thing I cared about in the world at that moment was finding the sonofabitch who'd shoved Jody Powers down the service elevator shaft. Jerry Dodd, our security chief, was with Chambrun when I arrived and they seemed to be totally involved in the murder of Teddy-boy Valentine. What town am I in? I found I really didn't give a damn about Valentine, or Sharon Brand, or the three-year-old disappearance of Victor Lewis. How had Jody been persuaded to leave the guest lounge backstage at the Thomas Show and go onto the service elevator? If someone had tried to force her to go, she could have screamed. It would have disrupted Dick Thomas's routines, but there were twenty-five or thirty people right there to help. She must have believed that someone had something of importance to tell her and had gone with him willingly. Once they were one floor above the ballroom on that service elevator, she could have screamed her lungs out and no one would have heard her. But who could have persuaded her, tricked her into going? It had to be someone she trusted, or at least someone she felt certain could supply her with information she'd gone backstage to find. I wished to God she hadn't trusted her memory for "dirt" about people, had put down everything in her files. I might be getting somewhere if it had been that way.

Hardy was a little more nearly in my region than Chambrun and Jerry. He had spent the last three hours interrogating the Thomas Show people and the guests. He had come up empty. Not one person admitted to having seen Jody leave the guest lounge or go aboard the service elevator with someone. Sally Cleaves, the singer, was the last person to see Jody alive in the lounge. Jody had been gone when the next guest, the child abuse expert, Dr. Snodgrass, had gone into the lounge to wait for his cue, if the doctor was telling the truth, and why shouldn't he be?

Hardy appeared in Chambrun's office almost immediately after I'd arrived, and before I'd had a chance to get Chambrun and Jerry off the Valentine case and into my league. With the detective was Lou Feldman, the producer of the Dick Thomas Show. Feldman was a small dark man whose ancestors must have come from Middle Europe somewhere. What does the producer of a television show do? He's like the contractor on a construction job. He assembles all the workmen, the masons, the steel erectors, the carpenters, the electricians; all the materials, the steel, the bricks, the mortar; the trucks to transport the men and materials; arranges the payroll—and on and on. In Feldman's case he arranged for the place where the show would be staged, in different cities all over the country, he handled everyone's transportation, camera crew, lighting experts, scenic designers, Dick Thomas's researchers,

Jake Floyd and his band, guests, public relations people. He was responsible for assembling all the pieces in the right place at the right time, but he had nothing to do with staging the show. That was in the hands of the director, Dick Thomas himself, the head cameraman, the lighting and sound men.

Lou Feldman was a worried man that evening.

"We've got problems, Mr. Chambrun," he said.

"An understatement, I should think," Chambrun said. He sat at his desk, eyes narrowed against the smoke from one of his Egyptian cigarettes. "I imagine you're aware that we, also, have problems."

"I feel we should cancel out the rest of the week here at the Beaumont," Feldman said. "Do the show from a TV studio somewhere without an audience."

"The audience is half your show," Chambrun said.

"Not the kind of audience we're going to get for the next few days," Feldman said. "Maniacs hoping to see more blood spilled."

Chambrun glanced at Hardy. "I take it you don't want the show moved, Lieutenant."

"I haven't scratched the surface of this thing yet," the detective said. "I haven't had a chance to study Miss Powers' files. I want these people to stay where they are, where after this first shock they may start to remember things they've forgotten today. Move them somewhere else and some of them may not be needed, will disappear. If Feldman tries to move the show, I'll place every damn one of them under arrest, if I have to clean out a city jail to house them."

"Press crowding around us, trying to get in the act," Feldman said.

"That will happen anywhere you go, Mr. Feldman," Chambrun said. "I think we can control the crowds in the lobby. You can be a little more selective about your audience, if you choose. The lieutenant has a point, you know. Change the locale, and the chance that someone will recall something will fade away."

"I'd like to consider my options," Feldman said.

"You don't have any options, Mr. Feldman," Hardy said. "The show goes on here tomorrow or it doesn't go on at all."

"I'd better get back to Dick Thomas and tell him," Feldman said. "How can he do a show here without referring to what's happened? It'll change everything that's been set up."

"That might make the show more interesting," Chambrun said, smiling a tight little smile.

WHEN FELDMAN HAD gone, Hardy asked me about the Powers files. I told him they weren't going to be the gold mine we'd hoped for. The juicy information Jody might have had about people had never been put on paper. She kept all that in her head, in her "computer." The files contained only birth dates, education, career histories.

"By the way," I said, "does the name Claudine Trudeau mean anything to any of you?"

No one registered. I explained that a skimpy file on Miss Trudeau had been on Jody's desk along with the ones on Sharon Brand and Ted Valentine.

"The indexes in the files don't show any connection between this Trudeau dame and Sharon or Valentine. A vague thing. Rex Hilliard, the actor, was playing in stock in 1970. The Trudeau girl was an apprentice at the theater—some place in Connecticut. Hilliard took her back to Hollywood with him and got her a job at Universal."

"Screwing her way to a movie career," Jerry Dodd said.

"I said there was a vague connection," I said. "Hilliard played in four movies with Sharon Brand."

"And was her lover sometime in the mid-seventies," Chambrun said. "Not a secret. Sharon was never secretive about her men."

"Before Vic Lewis?" I asked.

"Yes. Victor Lewis came after Hilliard. No one after Lewis until Ted Valentine came into the picture."

"The Trudeau girl committed suicide in 1974," I said. "According to Jody's notes she just walked out into the ocean and drowned herself. It probably has no connection with our troubles. Jody must have dug out the file for some reason, some item for her column. While she had it out, she got the news about Valentine and went for his file and Sharon's without bothering to put the Trudeau file back."

"Maybe," Chambrun said. "But I don't like loose ends, do you, Hardy? We may be in luck. Rex Hilliard's in the previews of a play that's going to open on Broadway next week." He glanced at his watch. "Curtain should go down in about forty-five minutes. Maybe you could have Hilliard brought over here, Hardy. He might be able to explain away Claudine Trudeau."

"Can do," Hardy said. "What about Miss Brand? If this Trudeau woman fits into the picture somewhere, wouldn't she know?"

"Might," Chambrun said. He picked up his phone and asked to be connected with Fourteen B. He switched on the squawk box so we could all hear. "Sharon? Pierre. I wonder if I could come up and talk to you for a few minutes."

"It might keep me from dying of boredom," Sharon's husky voice replied. "Is there something new?"

"Maybe. Mark and I will join you in a few minutes."

"You need me?" I asked when he'd disconnected.

"To prevent you from emulating Stephen Leacock's hero who rode off in all directions at once," Chambrun said.

Sharon, wearing a wine-red housecoat, looked as if she was ready to go on camera. I don't imagine she was ever caught looking anything less than stunning.

Sergeant Croft had been replaced as Sharon's watchdog. The young policeman, sitting on a stool in the kitchenette, seemed just a little bit awestruck by his assignment. I suppose when he was a kid going to a double feature at the local movie house on a Saturday afternoon, the lady he was now guarding had been the most romantic of all heroines. I have to confess I had something of that same feeling when I looked at her. In a fantasy world I suppose I'd been just a little bit in love with her ever since I'd been old enough to think about such things.

Not in love with this real woman, though, but with an image created by a skillful actress out of material created by skillful writers. I reminded myself of that as I sat down in one of the chairs across a coffee table from the couch where she and Chambrun sat together. Who and what was the real Sharon Brand? Was she the woman I had seen last night in a frenzy of anger and wounded vanity, tossing chinaware around the Blue Lagoon? Was she the woman who had burst into genuine tears when she'd discovered Ted Valentine's belongings were gone from the suite, forcing her to assume he had left her? Or was she the woman who had taken the news of his violent death as though it was an item in a newspaper about a stranger? Was she the older woman, genuinely in love with young Victor Lewis, who had really been hurt by his disappearance and spent a small fortune trying to find him, who tried in the end to replace him with another young man who turned out to be a no-good?

I don't like to have my romantic fantasies muddled. I don't like finding out that a Joan Crawford, most sophisticated of heroines, was, according to her daughter, a monster. I wasn't sure I wanted to find out any truths about Sharon Brand. One young lover had disappeared and was presumed dead, at least by Chambrun and Jody Powers; another had been brutally murdered; and Jody, searching for the truth, had been equally brutally murdered. What kind of woman could be at the center of that violent vortex?

She looked so lovely, so relaxed, so coolly at ease. She didn't want to be bored to death, she had said on the phone. My God, I thought, what kind of reaction was that to what had happened in the last hours?

"I was shocked," she said, not sounding shocked, "to hear about Jody Powers. I met her several times in the last few years, beginning with the time when—when Victor disappeared. She did a piece about Vic and me, one of the few that didn't make an older woman-younger man relationship sound snide and distasteful. She understood, I think. I don't think she ever printed gossip that hurt people just to sell newspapers."

Chambrun let her have it. "She thought, as I do, that there is some connection between Vic Lewis's disappearance and Valentine's death. She also thought there was a tie-in with the Dick Thomas Show. That's what she was doing backstage this afternoon, looking for a clue. That, we think, is why she was killed.''

"How awful, but does it make sense?'' Sharon asked. ''Vic was involved with Lou Feldman and the Dick Thomas people at the time of—of his disappearance. I was letting him get his feet wet at managing my affairs.''

"You weren't satisfied with Ray Baxter?'' Chambrun asked.

"Red is the best,'' she said. She turned her head away. ''But I was in love with Vic. We expected to be together forever.''

She wasn't acting, I thought. She was telling us something real.

"But Teddy had no interest in Dick Thomas, or anything else connected with show business,'' Sharon went on, an edge on her voice. ''He didn't know Dick or any of his people that I'm aware of. He wouldn't even come to a rehearsal. I knew there'd be questions about my relationship with another young man. Such a big deal has been made of it ever since Vic. He just laughed and asked if I expected him to tell the American public how good I was in bed. 'Which is the only reason I have for hanging around you,' he said. I knew we were coming to the end of the line. I wasn't really sorry, Pierre, but I wanted to make the move, damn him!''

"He certainly didn't plan to leave the way he did,'' Chambrun said.

"Where are his things, his clothes and personal belongings?'' she asked, her voice harsh.

"The police are searching.''

"When they find them, they'll know where he planned to hole in,'' Sharon said.

"I wonder," Chambrun said. He shifted his position on the couch. "I came up here to ask you what may be a meaningless question, Sharon. Do you happen to know anything about a girl named Claudine Trudeau?"

"Oh my God!" Sharon laughed, sharp and humorless. "That tramp!"

"You knew her, then?"

"Not really. But we played a scandalous little scene together."

Chambrun waited for her to go on.

"I have reason to remember that it was six years ago—1974," Sharon said. "Vic and I were having dinner at the Brown Derby in Hollywood. Suddenly this red-haired tootsie I'd never laid eyes on in my life walked up to the table, picked up a cup of consommé I was having, and threw the hot soup right in my face. She called me an 'old whore.'" Sharon drew a deep breath. "The place went wild, of course—people dragging her away. Vic was trying to clean me up. He thought I might be badly burned. He should have known you don't get really hot soup in a restaurant. I didn't know who the girl was, or what her name was. I recall hearing the maitre d' as he dragged her off. 'You damn fool, don't you know you've just ruined your chances in this town forever?' Later he came to apologize and told us the girl's name was Claudine Trudeau, a bit player at Universal. That was that until the next morning."

"And then?"

"The next morning Vic brought me the morning paper. Claudine Trudeau had left the Brown Derby the night before, gone down to the ocean, and, like a character in a B movie, had walked out into the water and drowned herself.''

"And you didn't know why, or why she'd attacked you?"

"The police came to question me," Sharon said. "I didn't know the girl, but they knew something about her. It seems Rex Hilliard had brought her to Hollywood three or four years before that. She'd been in some play he was in. I don't think it's a secret, Pierre, that Rex and I were a thing in 1972 or there, just before Vic. It seems he was shacked up with the Trudeau girl about the time he decided I would be more fun—and more advantageous to his career. That, it seems, is why she had it in for me. That's all I know about her. Why are you asking me about her?"

Chambrun told her about finding the Trudeau file on Jody's desk. Jody had been interested in it at the moment she got the news about Ted Valentine's murder.

"It draws a blank for me, Pierre. I haven't had a thought about Claudine Trudeau for a long time—years."

"Lieutenant Hardy is having Hilliard brought here to question him about the girl," Chambrun said. "If Hilliard lived with Claudine, he may know why Jody would have been interested in her so long after her suicide."

"If Rex can remember," Sharon said. "There have been so many women in his life." She laughed. "He can almost match me for changing partners, Pierre."

REX HILLIARD was in Chambrun's office with Hardy when we got back there. He looked tired and older than

I thought he would look. I guess makeup for camera and stage obliterated the lines in his face and neck.

He knew Chambrun. He was a not infrequent customer in our bars and restaurants when he was in town.

"The lieutenant has been asking me about Claudine," he said to Chambrun. He had a deep, well-controlled voice—an actor's voice. "After all these years it seems wild she should come onstage again."

"It seems Claudine Trudeau wasn't her real name," Hardy said.

"No more French than my Aunt Sally," Jody had written on the girl's file.

"Like a lot of stage-struck kids, she invented a name for herself," Hilliard said. "A lot of junk about being born in France. She thought it would glamorize her. She overlooked the fact that she needed to be able to act to make it."

"What was her real name, do you know?" Chambrun asked.

"Would you believe I don't remember if I ever knew," Hilliard said. "Unpronounceable Polish, if I recall. I called her 'Bunny.'" Hilliard's smile was wry. "She had certain talents that reminded me of a rabbit. I simply don't understand the interest in her now, Mr. Chambrun. The poor kid's been dead for six years!"

"It's Jody Powers' interest in her after six years that interests us," Chambrun said.

"As you get older, the passage of time speeds up," Hilliard said, scowling at a cigarette he was tapping on the back of his hand. I recognized the symptoms of a man who's trying to stop smoking. He doesn't light it, but he plays with it. "It's rather frightening to look back and recall how much time out of my life I gave to that girl. 1970 to 1973. She was an apprentice at a summer theater, I was a guest star, a name. Kids made a big fuss over me. This one kid, Bunny Trudeau, was so physically beautiful, so lush, it hurt—and so willing!'' Hilliard shook his head as he remembered. ''I was in my mid-forties, she was about nineteen. Bad time of life for an aging male, I suppose. She made me feel like a giant for a while. When that summer stock job was over, she begged me to take her to Hollywood. God knows she was beautiful enough to look at to give her a chance. But she was so *dumb*! When she opened her mouth to talk about anything, you wanted to run, not walk, to the nearest way out. So I took her to Hollywood, and I settled her into an apartment, and it was rather fun to show her off to the brotherhood out there. But any kind of social life was embarrassing. She was so stupid!'' He put the unlighted cigarette in his mouth and then snatched it away as though it had burned him. ''I gave almost thee years of my time to that dumb broad. Then, in 1973, I went on location to make a film with Sharon Brand. *Downhill is the Way to the Top*. One of Sharon's best. She and I got together.'' He looked steadily at Chambrun. ''I'm not gossiping, or boasting, Mr. Chambrun. Sharon and I became an 'item' quite openly. And what a relief! At last here was someone with whom I could carry on an intelligent conversation, who was a professional peer, a very dear person, actually.

''Well, I am not a total heel, gentlemen. I went back to Bunny Trudeau and told her the ball game was over. I made some financial arrangements so that she wouldn't starve to death. There wasn't any question that some other guy could be as easily bowled over by her sexual charms as I had been. There was no chance she would have to be lonely. She cried and carried on, but I didn't think it was a lost lover that was bothering her. She had seen me as the most likely person to force a break for her in the film business. No way. She photographed like a dream, but unless she could find a part as deaf-mute, she didn't have a chance. She just couldn't read the simplest line to save her life."

"But she did make some films?" Chambrun asked.

"Yes, but except for the first one—a beach-boy saga in which she appeared only in a bikini—no real parts. Just decoration; a girl in a crowd, a model in a fashion show. She made a couple of hysterical attempts to persuade me to come back to her. One thing about me, Mr. Chambrun, I never go back. There is no way to mend old fences. I went on with Sharon for about a year, and then I had to go to Rome to make a film. It meant a four to six month separation. One night I got an overseas phone call from her. She'd gotten herself involved with Victor Lewis, a man young enough to be her son. It was for real, she told me. She was grateful to me for all the fun we'd had together. Good-bye." The unlit cigarette broke in two in his fingers. "Well, I was grateful, and I thanked her, and that was that." He drew a deep breath. "I was still in Rome when Bunny Trudeau played her last big scene."

"The Brown Derby? Sharon just told us about it," Chambrun said.

"Soup in the face of the lady who had stolen me from her. I suppose that was the way she saw it. She couldn't imagine that I'd been bored to distraction by her. And then the *A Star Is Born* finale: a walk into the ocean until the cold waters swallowed her up. A Hollywood ending for someone who couldn't make Hollywood."

"And that's it?"

Hilliard nodded. "No family ever turned up to claim the body. I wired money for a simple burial. And that's it."

"Do you know of any connection Claudine Trudeau may have had with the Dick Thomas Show?" Chambrun asked.

Hilliard looked surprised. "Good God, no," he said. "She never did anything important enough to rate an interview; she didn't sing, or dance, or perform."

"A boyfriend on the show before, during, or after her time with you?"

"Not before, not during," Hilliard said. "I can't answer for after."

"Girl friends who might know?"

"None who ever came into my life," Hilliard said. "It's a sad thing, Mr. Chambrun, no matter how lacking in quality a person may be, to have not a single friend to care when you die. No one turned up for Bunny's funeral. Just a body in a box, in an unmarked grave—until I arranged for a headstone when I got back, and put a bunch of flowers on the grass—once."

But Jody Powers had kept a file on her!

FOUR

I NEVER SEE Jake Floyd that I'm not reminded of the old gag about the man who meets an old friend on the street and is asked how things are going. "Well, I'm working for the local gossip columnist, but don't tell my mother if you see her. She thinks I play the piano in a house of ill repute."

That's where Jake had begun, bald when he was twenty, unlit cigar stuck in the corner of his mouth, a hundred bucks on the line if he couldn't play a requested tune. At age forty he had found a home with the Dick Thomas Show. Five days a week he improvised, accompanied, and made musical comments. At his special kind of work he is the greatest. There was nothing of the romantic or the poet about Jake at age sixty. He'd been with Dick Thomas for twenty years and he was still a street urchin who had lived his life to a jazz beat. But I suspected that under his tough, cigar-chewing exterior he was as soft inside as Louisa May Alcott.

I ran across Jake in the Trapeze Bar about midnight. The Trapeze is located at the mezzanine level above the Beaumont's lobby. Some Alexander Calder type artist had decorated it with mobiles of circus performers on trapezes. A faint movement of air from the air conditioning system keeps those mobiles in constant, gentle motion. The Trapeze is an oasis for people who like to drink while they talk, and after two of Eddie the bartender's dry martinis you could get the notion that the whole place was swinging in space.

One of my regular chores was to check out the bars, the restaurants, and the Blue Lagoon each night. I have described it somewhere as being like Marshal Dillon putting Dodge City to bed each night. Was there anyone who needed special attention? Was anyone threatening to make trouble? Was the general atmosphere what it was intended to be? Sometimes Chambrun took over for me, but tonight he was still closeted with Lieutenant Hardy in his office.

Jake Floyd was sitting at a corner table alone, cigar stuck out of the corner of his mouth at an aggressive angle, his bald head shining in the light from a chandelier located almost directly over him.

"How goes it?" I asked him.

The cigar moved over to the other corner of his mouth. "Crocked to the gills," he said. "Is there any law against it?" He beckoned to a waiter. "Once more for me and whatever my friend wants."

The waiter knew about me and Jack Daniel's. He didn't ask.

"Your cop friend find anything in the garbage?" Jake asked as I sat down in a chair across the table from him.

"Not that he's talking about," I said.

"He thinks someone saw someone drag the Powers girl out of the guest lounge by the hair of her head and forgot all about it? That's what I call 'cop thinking.' I thought they were going to move the show out of here for the rest of the week, but Lou Feldman was just here and said the police say 'no.' It couldn't matter less to me. Your cop friend can ask me twenty times a day what I saw and the answer would still be 'nothing.' At the end of four days the guy who killed the chick can be in China, and the answer will still be 'nothing.' She was okay after the show had started. Do you know that for the hour and a half after the show goes on the air I don't have one second in which I'm not up to my ass in it. I wouldn't notice if somebody drove a caterpillar tractor on backstage.''

"So your conscience is clear," I said.

The waiter brought our drinks. Jake was drinking gin on the rocks with a splash of grenadine in it. "Whores taught me to drink this in my dearly days," he said. "For them it would be colored water most of the time, with the customer paying for booze. I had to keep my wits about me in those days with a hundred bucks on the line if I didn't know a tune. Since then it's always been gin. What's the line from the English play? 'Gin is mothers' milk to me.'''

"*Pygmalion,*" I said.

"Who?"

"George Bernard Shaw's *Pygmalion*. The tea party scene."

"I guess I never saw it. Just heard the line," Jake said.

"They made *My Fair Lady*, the musical, out of it," I said.

That rang a bell. "'Get Me to the Church on Time,'" he said. "Old Stanley Holloway. 'I Could Have Danced All Night'—Julie Andrews. Good tunes in that show." The cigar crossed his lips again. "But gin never made a fair lady out of anyone." He laughed at his own joke.

He remembered people, names. I tried one out on him. "You ever run into a girl named Claudine Trudeau?" I asked him.

"Sure," he said. "Ex-wife of the Prime Minister of Canada, isn't she?"

"Not this one," I said. "Same last name. This one committed suicide in Hollywood about six years ago. Actress who couldn't act. Lived for a while with an actor named Rex Hilliard."

Jake's pale blue eyes narrowed. He was looking into the past somewhere.

"Claudine Trudeau wasn't her real name," I said. "She was Polish."

Jake smiled at me. "You know why Polish dogs have bumps on their heads?" he asked.

"No," I said patiently.

"From chasing parked cars," he said. That one convulsed him.

"I think the Powers girl thought Claudine Trudeau had some connection with the Dick Thomas operation," I said.

"As I remember, Los Angeles cops had the same idea about this Claudette," Jake said.

"Claudine," I said. "The Los Angeles cops—?"

"We were doing the show in Dallas the week this Claudine chick played her big scene," Jake said. "For some reason the Los Angeles cops thought she had some connection with someone on our show. Sent a man to Dallas with pictures of her."

"So no one knew her?"

Jake shook his head. "I never laid eyes on the girl in the pictures. Never heard that name—Claudette What-have-you. We do the show in a different city every week, you know, Mark? Most of us don't have any home; live out of suitcases. The boys in the band, six of 'em, I know. They're my responsibility. They're like sailors—girls in every port. We play Hollywood twice a year. But no one on the show knew this Claudette."

"Claudine."

"Hell, man, she's been dead for six years. It seems longer ago than that."

"Nineteen seventy-four," I said.

"What could she have to do with what happened today—yesterday?"

"I wish I knew," I said.

THE BEAUMONT seemed normal, quiet, that early morning. I suspect there was a lot of unusual talk about murder, but no hysteria. I checked on the Spartan Bar. This is the room the ardent feminists don't like. The customers are mostly old gents playing dominoes, gin, backgammon, and occasionally chess. Mr. Quiller, the maitre d', discourages ladies. Turn up there with a girl and you're likely to be told, politely, that all the tables are reserved.

Dr. Partridge, our elderly house physician, is always in the Spartan Room about one in the morning. He waits for Chambrun to show up for a game of backgammon. He's been dreaming of beating Chambrun at the board for about fifteen years. Chambrun is hell on wheels at the game and I don't think the doctor has ever taken him.

The doctor was standing at the bar, looking fretful.

"I don't suppose Pierre will show up tonight," he said. "People killing people."

"He wants to make sure there are no more," I said.

Partridge gave me something close to a look of sympathy. "Girl who went down the elevator shaft was a friend of yours, Mark?"

"Yes."

"A mess," the doctor said. "I've seen the Medical Examiner's report. She was so smashed up by that fall there's no way to tell whether that killed her, or whether she was slugged to death first—like that fellow in the alley."

"That's possible?" I asked, feeling a chill along my spine.

"No way to tell for sure," Partridge said. "Either way, Mark, it must have been quick."

"Is that supposed to make me feel better?"

"If you'd seen people die slowly as often as I have," the doctor said, "it would."

Mr. Quiller came over to tell me that Chambrun wanted me up in his office. The Man was still at it. I glanced at the clock over the bar and saw that it was twenty minutes to two. It was not late for Chambrun to be up. Trying to fit sleep into his schedule, I'd long since decided that six hours was his average maximum. He seemed to be able to thrive on it. Not me. After a week of those hours I'd have to retire for a few days to catch up.

I walked past the Carnation Room on my way to the elevators. Four reporters were involved in a game of bridge. I supposed they had agreed to contact the competition if anything broke. Not everyone could stand watch all night. One of the bridge players spotted me in the doorway and started to rise, but I signaled him there was nothing.

Betsy Ruysdale, The Man's secretary, has no regular hours. When she senses she is needed, professionally, she is there. She looked as fresh as she did every morning at breakfast.

"Ray Baxter, Sharon Brand's agent and manager," she said, pointing toward the inner sanctum.

I remembered Baxter had been due in at Kennedy about one o'clock. He'd evidently come straight to the Beaumont on the double. Chambrun had anticipated that, and when Baxter had asked for Sharon at the front desk, he'd been switched on to The Man.

The flaming red hair, worn mod-long, explained Baxter's nickname. It was startling and, I decided, real. I suppose he was in his mid-fifties, but he had an athletic, vigorous look to him—a tough, square jaw, very shrewd gray-green eyes. He shook hands hard and I only just managed to keep my knees from buckling.

"Hell of a day for all of you," he said. "When I got the news on the plane about Jody Powers, I couldn't believe it. Two in one day! Mr. Chambrun tells me that Sharon is bearing up well."

"You and Mr. Chambrun know her better than I do," I said. "I can't be sure when she is reacting normally and when she is just acting. She's in control anyway."

"She's spent the last thirty years braced against the certainty of being swarmed under by the press, columnists, talk-show jocks, studio P.R. people. All she has to do is flutter an eyelid and it's news. Hard to live with that in a crisis."

"That's why Mr. Baxter is here," Chambrun said. He was, as usual, at his desk, a demitasse of Turkish coffee beside him. Ruysdale had evidently made Baxter a drink. It looked like Scotch and soda as he turned the glass around in strong, square fingers.

"I am composed of a few parts compassion and a great many parts practicality," Baxter said. "Sharon is a friend in trouble, but she is also my major meal ticket. My whole stable of clients is a result of my success with Sharon's career. I owe her." He smiled.

"Right now my bread is buttered here in the Beaumont. But also a good friend needs my support."

"Right now we are floating around in a world of theories," Chambrun said. He held his lighter to a cigarette and the flame illuminated his dark, thoughtful face. "Two and two make four, or five, or six at the moment. Coincidences make clouds."

"Coincidences?"

"The lady's two young lovers wiped out less than three years apart," Chambrun said. "Both disasters occur when she's involved with the Dick Thomas Show. Jody Powers believed there was a connection and died. She was interested in a file she had on a girl who committed suicide six years ago who once threw a cup of hot soup in Sharon's face in public. Sharon is tied into everything we touch, but how?"

"Claudine Trudeau!" Baxter said.

"So that registers with you, Mr. Baxter."

"Look, everyone calls me 'Red,'" Baxter said. "Let's not be formal."

"So that registers with you, Red," Chambrun said.

Baxter moved restlessly around, drink in hand. "My job for Sharon is not just negotiating contracts. Her public image is important, an asset if it's good. In the old days in Hollywood a star's private life was a carefully guarded secret. Your reputation stayed entirely pure or the Goldwyns and the Mayers threw the book at you. Things are different now. People live together without marriage and nobody interferes. The gossip columnists make a living from it. For the last fifteen years Sharon's private life has been a public delight. There have been more men in her life than I can count. She has been perfectly open about it. Six or more years ago when she first became involved with Vic Lewis it became almost a cause. Older women all over the place began gunning for young studs. They quoted Sharon by the yard. 'Age has nothing to do with love, tenderness, sharing.' It didn't, as far as Sharon was concerned with Vic Lewis. He was a nice boy, a decent boy, very much in love with Sharon, and why not?''

"You don't believe he walked out on her?"

"Never," Baxter said. "Something he couldn't prevent happened to him. God knows what. The cops and Sharon's private eyes never came up with anything. But for sure, Vic Lewis never deserted her."

"Do we come up with Claudine Trudeau soon?" Chambrun asked. I knew the slight rasp of irritation when he spoke.

"That crazy scene in the Brown Derby made news, of course," Baxter said. "The next day, when it was discovered the girl had committed suicide, it was big news. The cops did a pretty fair job on it. They believed Sharon when she said she'd never laid eyes on the girl before. They dug and dug and came up with what I believe was the answer. Back, ten years ago—1970—this Claudine Trudeau became Rex Hilliard's live-in pal. After a little more than two years Hilliard dumped the girl and took up with Sharon. The Trudeau girl tried to make it on her own, found herself some other guys, but never got over Rex. Then Sharon gave Rex the gate and took up with Vic Lewis. Sharon, to the Trudeau girl, was the villain of the piece. I suspect Rex wouldn't take her back when the thing with Sharon was over. So—hot soup in the face, publicly naming Sharon a whore, and out into the ocean and down for the third time."

"I had already put that together," Chambrun said, drumming with his fingers on the edge of the desk.

"I was concerned for Sharon," Baxter said. "I was afraid some friend or member of the Trudeau girl's family would show up and start throwing dirt around. No one ever did; no friend, no relative. Rex Hilliard paid for her funeral, not being a complete louse."

"Did you ever find out what her real name was? Her family's name?"

"It never surfaced," Baxter said. "The police questioned a few guys she'd been intimate with after Hilliard left her. They didn't know. Hilliard claimed he didn't know."

"Something Polish, unpronounceable," Chambrun said.

"You've talked to Rex?"

"Just before you came," Chambrun said. "You know the Hollywood scene, Red, as well as anyone alive. Why would Jody Powers be interesting herself in a sketchy file about a girl who committed suicide out there six years ago? Jody was a very modern newspaperwoman whose column was geared to today, to now, to the moment. What could have interested her about a girl who never made it at all, who committed suicide six years ago, and whose chief claim to any attention is that she was a live-in friend of Rex Hilliard's, and on the day she killed herself she threw a cup of soup in Sharon's face?"

Baxter shook his head slowly. "There aren't three people in Hollywood who would know who you were talking about if you mentioned the girl's name," he said. "She was never known except, you might say, for a day. Forgotten. Gone."

"Yet Jody Powers kept a file on her," Chambrun said.

With damn little in it, I said. "What was special to Jody about Claudine Trudeau she kept in her head!" Over and over, round and round, I thought.

"Jody Powers believed, as you do, Red," Chambrun said to Baxter, "that Vic Lewis never walked out on Sharon. She believed something happened to him. Could she have thought Claudine Trudeau had anything to do with Lewis's disappearance?"

"Get your dates straight, boss," I said, starting to seethe a little. "The Trudeau girl had been dead three years when Vic Lewis vanished."

"I'm well aware of that," Chambrun said. "But Jody Powers kept the girl alive in her file. There has to have been a reason."

Red Baxter put his empty drink glass down on the corner of Chambrun's desk rather pointedly, I thought. Chambrun signaled to me and I took the glass over to the sideboard and made the agent a fresh Scotch and soda.

"Let's get around to what must concern you, Red," Chambrun said as I brought the drink back.

"Meaning?"

"Sharon. You flew East the minute you heard the news about Ted Valentine, without letting Sharon know you were coming."

"I tried to reach her," Baxter said. "I couldn't get through to her. I suppose the cops were interrogating her. I got a plane reservation, so I just came."

"Because you were concerned about her?"

"Of course."

"You thought she might not be safe?"

"Safe from what?" Baxter asked, frowning.

"There's a policeman up in Sharon's suite with her," Chambrun said. "Lieutenant Hardy and I both thought the murder of Ted Valentine was meant to hurt her, just as the disappearance of Vic Lewis hurt her. Some kind of psycho at work. And his next move could be right at Sharon herself."

"My God!" Baxter said.

"Who could resent Sharon's young lovers? Resent her for having them? Someone out of her past? Rex Hilliard, someone before him? And the timing, Red, connected each time with the Dick Thomas Show? The last time she was on the Dick Thomas Show Vic Lewis disappeared. The next time was to have been yesterday, and Ted Valentine was beaten to death. Does that suggest anything to you, Red?"

Something clicked in my head and I came out with it. I told them about my conversation with Jake Floyd. "None of the people on the Dick Thomas Show stay in the same place for more than a week," I said. "Always traveling, different city every week. That staff and crew haven't been in the same place with Sharon since the last time—the day Vic Lewis disappeared."

"And they won't be in the same place again for a long time—after this week is finished," Chambrun said.

"So we get her the hell out of New York!" Baxter almost shouted.

"And wait, with no leads, for someone to strike at her again?" Chambrun asked.

"You want to set her up for this psycho during the next four days?" Baxter said. Color had faded from his tanned face.

"I think that's a decision for Sharon to make for herself," Chambrun said. "We can protect her here. If we nail our man, she can go about her business and breathe again. If she leaves the hotel, leaves town, he will just relax and wait for his next chance to have at her. And now she'll know that she's a target and she won't have a moment's peace. That would be an unpleasant way for her to live out whatever time she has left."

"Oh, brother!" Baxter said, and gulped at his drink.

MY APARTMENT is on the same floor as Chambrun's office. I have two rooms, a kitchenette, and bath. My office is just two doors further down the corridor. I would have enjoyed living in one of the penthouses on the roof, like The Man, but the theory was, I guess, that I was never more than a minute away from the center of activity if I was needed. The location was a little public if I wanted to keep my private life private.

That night, feeling that I would almost certainly fall asleep on my feet if I didn't hit the sack, I headed almost eagerly for my bed. My last instructions from Chambrun were to be at the ready at nine-thirty in the morning as usual. He had arranged with Dick Thomas to have a filming of yesterday's show, so that he and Hardy could see every moment of the hour and a half as it had gone out to the public TV sets in the area, and would be seen at different times on the syndicated stations across the country. Dick Thomas's staff people would be present to make certain that nothing unusual had been caught by the cameras which had been overlooked at the time. The filming was to take place in the ballroom. We would go there after Chambrun had finished his breakfast. Nothing could be allowed to interfere with his chicken hash, or steak, or chop, or creamed codfish on an English muffin. I think if a hydrogen bomb had been bearing down on us, Chambrun would have raised his hand and said, "Stop! Until after breakfast!" He would have expected obedience.

The second-floor corridor is not brightly lighted. There is no public traffic there. I was suddenly aware that someone was standing just outside my apartment as I approached. It was a man wearing gray slacks, a blue denim jacket, a yellow sports shirt open at the neck. His fair hair was crew cut and he was tanned the color of a mahogany sideboard, muscular. Something told me, warned me, that he wasn't lost. As I got close to him, I was aware of the coldest, most penetrating pale blue eyes I could ever remember seeing.

"Can I help you?" I asked him.

"You're Haskell?" he asked.

"Yes."

"You're the sonofabitch who took Jody to where she got killed," he said.

I sensed what was coming and I ducked and closed with him. The blow that had been meant for my jaw caught me on the side of the head and nearly finished me. But I managed to embrace him and hang on. He was strong, lithe, and I knew I was going to be no match for him. And then, just as quickly as it had begun, it was over. He just stopped trying, and waited for me to relinquish my bear hug.

"I'm sorry," he said in a flat, irrational voice. "I just had to lash out at someone. Did you know, Haskell, that Jody and I were to have been married next week?"

I backed away, breathing hard. "You're Captain Stryker? Ben Stryker?"

He nodded. "Nancy Armin told me where to find you."

"At nearly three in the morning?" I said, which didn't make much sense. It couldn't matter to him what time of day it was. He was hurting.

"Come on in," I said.

I unlocked my door, switched on the lights, and stood aside to let him in.

"Nightcap?" I suggested.

He shook his head. "I think I'd better try to stay organized," he said. "Get me started and I'm likely to begin taking apart every bastard on that Dick Thomas Show."

"I know how you feel," I said. "I was there myself earlier in the day."

"You cared for Jody?" he asked, and those pale eyes were a little unnerving.

"I cared for her," I said. "Not in your league, though. She was in and out of the hotel a lot, people she needed to see in her business spent time here. We had an occasional drink together, laughed, talked. I have pretty normal male impulses, Stryker. She made it very clear to me that—well, that she was involved elsewhere."

"Do you know where I was today—yesterday?"

"'Off,' according to Nancy."

He turned away. "I was buying a small house in Connecticut where Jody and I were going to spend our free time."

I didn't comment. I mean, what was there to say?

"The news, the incredible news, came on my car radio," he said. "I was going to kill someone."

"I know."

"I still am," he said.

"So you came looking for me?" My laugh sounded false.

"I'm sorry, again, that I took a swing at you. I just had to let loose on someone. You took her to where she died. Who makes sense at a time like this?"

"Not you—and not me," I said.

"Nancy said you were close to Pierre Chambrun and the cops."

"My job."

"I don't know quite where to begin," Stryker said, "because I don't know how much Jody told you. But Nancy Armin says you were on the same track about the connection between the Dick Thomas Show and the violence to Sharon Brand's young man. I mean that first young man, Vic Lewis." Stryker's smile was twisted. "The last time I talked to Jody was early yesterday morning. On the phone. She didn't know then about the second young man, Ted Valentine. There wasn't a hint of any trouble, any danger. I would be closing the deal for the house later. Everything was fine, everything was great. Then in the late morning— driving around with the car radio on—I heard about Valentine. No use trying to reach Jody. I—I knew her style. She'd be up to her ears in it—as a reporter, a newspaperwoman."

"A damn good one," I said.

"Too damn good," he said, his teeth gritted. "She must have come up with the answer. Right? She must have known too much."

"Except we don't know what she knew," I said. "She thought there was a connection between Vic Lewis's disappearance and the murder of Valentine. A connection between those two things and the Dick Thomas Show. She wanted me to take her backstage. I did, but when we got there, the show was about to start and they wouldn't let us circulate. We went to the guest lounge, and eventually I left her there. There were things I had to check. I may never forgive myself for that. But I swear, Ben, it never occurred to me she was in any danger while the show was going on. There was an army of people—''

''I know,'' he said. ''Could I—could I change my mind about a drink?''

''Sure. Name your poison.''

''A slug of brandy, if you happen to have any.''

I went into the kitchenette and poured him at shot of Hennessey. He had relaxed into an armchair when I brought it back to him. He drank almost half of it before he spoke again.

''Nancy told me about your visit to Jody's apartment,'' he said. ''About your interest in Jody's files.''

''They don't have the kind of stuff in them we hoped for,'' I said. ''Just biographical details. Any special stuff she kept in her head, it seems.''

''But not necessarily secret,'' Stryker said. ''She talked to me a lot about stories she was working on.'' He leaned forward. ''Nancy says you found three files on her typewriter: one on Sharon Brand, one on Ted Valentine, and one on Claudine Trudeau. You thought she'd had the Trudeau file out when the news came about Valentine.''

''Best explanation,'' I said.

''But wrong, I think,'' he said. ''She heard about Valentine and she dug out the three files she thought were pertinent. Claudine Trudeau had always been a part of her thinking about Vic Lewis's disappearance. Now another young lover gets the ax. She thinks of Trudeau again.''

''Six years dead,'' I said.

''But connected with the Dick Thomas Show.''

"How do you figure that?"

"Because I know something that isn't in the file," Stryker said. He sipped his drink.

"Do I have to pry it out of you?" I asked him.

"Jody never believed that Vic Lewis walked out on Sharon Brand," he said. "It was her kind of story and she stuck with it. Everything she could dig up about Sharon Brand was important. Among a mass of material was the story of Claudine Trudeau throwing a cup of soup in Sharon's face and calling her an 'old whore.' That had made some of the columns, particularly after the girl committed suicide the next day."

"Six years ago," I said again. "It was three years before anything happened to Vic Lewis."

"But three years ago Vic Lewis was very much involved with an appearance Sharon was to make on the Dick Thomas Show. He disappeared on the very day she was on the show."

"I know."

"This is what wasn't in Claudine Trudeau's file but which you can easily verify. The Los Angeles police have it in their files. When the girl committed suicide, they tried to find family, relatives, anyone connected with her. No family surfaced. Rex Hilliard, they learned, had been her lover before he dropped her and took up with Sharon Brand. He was in Rome making a film. I guess they talked on the overseas phone with him but he wasn't much help. They found out where she was living—a dingy little apartment somewhere in Hollywood. There was nothing there about family or friends, no address book. But they found something that Jody never forgot. It was an itinerary of the Dick Thomas Show for the next six months."

"Itinerary?"

"A travel plan of every town and city the Dick Thomas Show would be in for the next six months—the studios, hotels, and theaters where the show would be done."

"Proving what?"

"Proving that Claudine Trudeau knew how to get in touch with someone on the Dick Thomas Show any time she wanted to for the next six months," Stryker said. "A boyfriend, a lover, a relative."

"Who?"

"Dead end," Stryker said. "The police found some studio photographs of Claudine in her apartment—the kind an actress leaves with a producer or an agent when she's looking for a job. Good, clear, unmistakable likenesses of the girl. They took them to the Dick Thomas Show, wherever they were at the time, and showed them around. Nobody on the show admitted to knowing her or ever having seen her before. No one had an answer as to why she had the travel plans. But she had them."

"And so, when a second violence turns up on the show—"

"Jody thinks about Claudine Trudeau and takes out her file to look at it again," Stryker said.

"She was convinced there was a connection between the two violences," I said. "She wanted to go backstage to see how many familiar faces she would see from the time of Vic Lewis's disappearance. The cops and Pierre Chambrun think, too, there is a connection. That the real target is Sharon Brand."

"There is someone there who lied about not knowing Claudine Trudeau," Stryker said. "Someone who may hate Sharon Brand because of what she did to Claudine."

"Stealing away Rex Hilliard?"

"Right. Just as sure as God, Jody spotted that someone backstage yesterday and said something that set him off. And I'm going to get him!"

I knew how he felt. I'd been there myself a few hours back. I still wanted to get the man who'd destroyed Jody, but I wasn't thinking in terms of a personal violence anymore. Get him, and let the cops deal with him. But Stryker, if he got his hands on him, wasn't going to wait for the law to settle things. I understood his fierce need for vengeance. Jody had been much more to him than she had ever been to me. I had just dreamed about her. He had had her, loved her, planned for a life with her, and now he was ready to kill the man who had put an end to all that. Looking at him, I knew he wasn't just talking.

"It won't bring her back, you know," I said.

"In the last minutes of her life," Stryker said in a cold, hard voice, "she must have known what was going to happen to her, the trap she'd fallen into. She must have felt a kind of terror that can't be described. He's going to feel that same fear before I finally let him have it."

"She wouldn't want you to run that kind of risk just to punish him," I said.

"She doesn't have to look at him and do nothing," he said. "She doesn't have to live with everything that matters lost. Do you think I give a damn what happens to me after I've dealt with him?"

"She would care."

"But she isn't here!" He took me by the shoulders, shook me. "She isn't ever going to be here!"

PART THREE

ONE

UNDER ANY other circumstances I might not have slept after that session with Ben Stryker. Jody's airline pilot was almost certainly a second potential killer on the loose. I told myself that time might cool him off; that perhaps Chambrun and Hardy between them might talk some sense into him tomorrow. Right then I was almost too pooped to care. I scattered my clothes and fell into bed.

It seemed like minutes later, not four and a half hours, that my phone began to ring persistently. It was broad daylight and my bedside clock told me it was the switchboard calling to wake me, usual time, usual place. Ora Veach, chief operator on the switchboard, a motherly old bag with a formidable bosom, would keep at me till she was sure I was up and in motion.

I picked up the phone and muttered something.

"Up and at 'em, Tiger," Ora Veach said, with her disgusting early morning good cheer. "Mark?"

"Ugh," I said.

"There's a chick been trying to reach you for about half an hour. I told her I couldn't call you till eight fifteen. I knew you'd had a tough night. Girl's name is Nancy Armin. She says you know how to reach her."

"I know," I said. "Thanks, Ora."

"My pleasure. I'll call back in five minutes—just to make sure."

Like death and taxes, Ora Veach cannot be side-stepped. When it's her job to get you up, she gets you up.

I didn't have any other way to reach Nancy Armin except at Jody's apartment. She was there, sounding a little breathless.

"Oh, thanks for calling, Mark. I couldn't persuade the operator at the hotel to put me through."

"Mrs. Veach was just trying to let me have the last few minutes of a very short night," I said. "What's up?"

"Have you seen or had any contact with Ben—Captain Stryker?"

"I have," I said, "with a small lump on the side of my head to prove it."

"Oh God, Mark, he isn't rational," Nancy said.

"Yes and no," I said. "Mostly no. How he feels is understandable, but I don't think the police or my boss are going to take kindly to a one-man revenge crusade. It can get in the way."

"Are they getting anywhere—the police?"

"They have two crimes to solve," I told her. "In less than an hour we're looking at the master reel of yesterday's Dick Thomas Show. They hope the cameras may have picked up something."

"I'm coming over there. Someone's got to try to keep Ben from going haywire."

"If you can manage that, you may get a medal," I said.

Our Nancy, I thought, was a little more than naturally concerned about a man who had been about to marry her boss.

Chambrun couldn't have had much more sleep than I'd had, but he looked chipper and ready to go when I reported to him in his office. I told him about my encounter with Ben Stryker. He was still sitting at the breakfast table in his office, embarked on his second cup of American coffee. M. Fresney, the chef, brought me coffee from the sideboard. He suggested chicken hash or broiled lamb kidneys. I wasn't for food, but I was grateful for the coffee.

"Your Captain Stryker is viewing the film with us," Chambrun told me. "He had Jerry Dodd out of bed at four this morning—after he'd left you, obviously. To quote from the late President Johnson, Jerry thought it would be better to have Stryker inside the tent peeing out, then outside the tent peeing in. It's possible he may recognize someone who had interested Jody Powers in some special way. At least we may be able to sit on him if he gets obstreperous."

There was, of course, no audience in the ballroom when Chambrun and I got there, but the stage area was crowded. The entire staff and crew of the Dick Thomas Show had been ordered to be there, along with Johnny Molloy, the co-host for the week; Ross Lubelle, the *Dracula* actor; Sally Cleaves, the nightclub singer: Dr. Snodgrass, the child abuse expert; Buddy Sellers, the singer.

Hardy was waiting for us in the control booth, along with Dick Thomas, Tony Meador, the director, and Lou Feldman, the producer. There were three other nameless young men who were Meador's assistant directors.

Americans, as a people, are constantly involved with scientific marvels, use them in their daily lives, and have no notion at all of what really makes them work. I drive a car. I know where the gas goes in, and I have sense enough to ask to have my oil checked from time to time. The engine, which carries me thousands of miles a year, is a mystery to me beyond that. Millions of people watch the Dick Thomas Show five days a week without having the faintest idea of how it is made to work.

The control booth is enclosed, a wide glass panel fronting the stage. Meador and his three assistants sit facing four monitors, small TV screens. Above those four monitors is a larger screen.

"We have four cameras in operation during the show," Meador explained to those of us who were ignorant. "Each camera has its own monitor here—one, two, three, and four. As director I select the picture I want to use and it shows on that master monitor above the others. I may choose a close-up of Dick and his guest during an interview. When there is a singer, or dancer, or stand-up comic, I can choose a long shot, a close-up, a side view. What I choose is what shows on the master, what is recorded on the master reel. That master reel is the show, as it is seen live, and as it is shown in different places at different times later in syndication. The master reel is it."

"But the other cameras are taking pictures that the audience doesn't see?" Hardy asked.

"Taking pictures, but they aren't recorded," Meador said. "The only pictures that are recorded are the ones I select and that show on the master monitor and are transferred to the master reel."

"Let's say you choose a close-up of Thomas and a guest," Chambrun said. "The other three cameras are taking pictures but they aren't recorded, right?"

"Right," Meador said.

"So what we'll see are the shots you chose during the show yesterday, but we won't see what the other three cameras may have seen?"

"Right."

"There is no film to show what those other three cameras may have seen?"

"Only the master shots which will show up on the master reel," Meador said.

"Would the cameramen on those cameras whose shots you didn't select remember what they were shooting?"

Meador shrugged. "Unless it was something unusual."

"Like someone dropping his pants just as he was about to make an entrance," one of the assistants said.

"I think I know what you're getting at, Mr. Chambrun," Meador said. "You'd hoped that one of the cameras not selected by me as the show was on, might have picked up something backstage that isn't on the master reel."

"Precisely," Chambrun said.

"There'll be no record of it," Meador said. "The only thing recorded is what you'll see on the master reel. The police questioned all the cameramen yesterday. None of them remembers seeing Miss Powers going anywhere, being taken anywhere by someone. You won't see anything like that on the master reel. I know. I've looked at it once already this morning."

One of the cameras might have seen something, but we'd never know.

Chambrun sounded disappointed. "So, let's look at the master reel," he said.

"We're supposed to be rehearsing for today's show," Lou Feldman, the producer, said.

"I don't want to see the whole show," Chambrun said. "Just up to Dr. Snodgrass's entrance. Jody Powers was gone from the guest lounge then."

"Run it," Meador said.

The master monitor came alive. There was a shot of the Beaumont from the outside. There was the sound of applause from the unseen audience. Then the announcer's voice.

"From the Hotel Beaumont in New York City—the Dick Thomas Show!"

I had seen and heard all this from the guest lounge with Jody only yesterday.

"And here, your host and mine, Dick Thomas!"

The applause mounted. There was a shot of the audience, and then, through the center entrance, came Dick Thomas. Dick smiled, bowed. He turned to look at the band, and there was a shot of Jake Floyd, cigar in the corner of his mouth, and his six musicians, while they vamped the introduction for Thomas. And then the song—"I Get No Kick from Champagne."

There wasn't anything to look for, anything unusual, during the song. I'd been with Jody while it was sung. When Thomas had finished the number, he acknowledged the applause. Then he raised his hand.

"We'll be back in a moment," Thomas told the audience.

On come two commercials, already inserted in the master reel. What went on onstage while those commercials were shown didn't appear. But I was still with Jody in the guest lounge.

Back on the monitor came Dick Thomas.

"I'm fortunate this week to have as my co-host a great dancer, a great singer, star of *The Honey Man*, a great guy I'm proud to call my friend—Johnny Molloy!''

There was Johnny, smiling his charming, crooked smile. The applause was thunderous. Johnny looked away and there was another shot of Jake and his boys vamping the intro to "Top Hat, White Tie, and Tails." Then Johnny went into it, singing and dancing in his marvelous Fred Astaire style. They shot him close up, at a distance, from the side. All four cameras covered that routine. He was tremendous.

I felt a kind of tight feeling in my gut. While this had been going on yesterday, Jody and I had decided we weren't going to get anywhere sitting in the guest lounge. I had needed to contact Chambrun. I could hear her voice. *"I'll be somewhere around,"* she'd said. *"Maybe I can think of some way to twist Pete Banazak's arm."*

And I had left her, God help me.

The master monitor stayed alive, relentlessly. There was another break in the show action for the endless flow of commercials. Do you have trouble with hemorrhoids? Does your underarm deodorant stick to your shirt? And then, back to Dick Thomas and Johnny Molloy. They were seated together on the platform, stage left. It was interview time. I kept waiting for the camera to move, to show something on the set besides two over-enlarged faces. Meador, the director, had chosen to stay right on Dick Thomas and his guest. I consoled myself by remembering that Jody was still all right at this point in the show. Ross Lubelle, the actor, and Sally Cleaves, the singer, was still to come, and both of them had seen and talked with Jody in the guest lounge.

Johnny Molloy, on the film, was talking to Thomas about his beginning in show business, how he had won some amateur contest, gotten a job in the chorus of a Broadway musical, understudied the lead and, right out of a Hollywood script, had a chance to go on for him. He had done a tap dance that had made him. Could he do that dance for us now? He could—and did. Once more he was center stage. The cameras were active again. Meador had selected long shots, close-ups, and an angle shot that, for a moment, exposed a segment of the backstage. I saw Chambrun leaning forward. I could have told him Jody was still in the lounge. But even in that brief angled shot there was no view of the lounge.

Johnny finished his routine and we went into the "We'll be back in a moment" routine and more commercials. Dr. Welby talked about decaffeinated coffee. A bunch of kids wiped the juice from luscious hamburgers off their chins.

A fresh close-up of Dick Thomas brought us to the next introduction. Ross Lubelle, the dark, romantic-looking actor, came out the center entrance, shook hands with Thomas and Johnny Molloy, and sat down on the platform between them. There followed, in close-up and semi-close-ups, a discussion of the *Dracula* play in which Lubelle was appearing. They showed early film clips of Bela Lugosi, who had originated the role in films, another of a more recent film with Frank Langella and Laurence Olivier, and finally the latest with Ross Lubelle, bending over a beautiful blonde, about to take a bite out of her swanlike neck.

I kept thinking that while all this was being recorded on the master reel, Jody was still in the lounge talking with Sally Cleaves, who was due to appear next.

"We'll be back in a minute."

More commercials. I could feel tensions mounting. Sally Cleaves, the young nightclub singer, must be waiting just outside the center entrance. Jody was alone in the lounge, or was there already someone there with her? Someone persuading her to go to her death? I glanced at Chambrun. A little muscle was rippling along the line of his jaw. This was the crucial time and Meador's master reel showed us absolutely nothing.

More commercials about bad breath and Dr. Whos-is's cure for fallen arches, and then another close-up of Dick Thomas.

"In an age of rock, and country, and disco music," Thomas told us on film, "the ballad singer is almost a thing of the past. When you hear my next guest, you will wonder why. This is a singer whose artistry shines like the brightest star. Ladies and gentlemen, please welcome—Sally Cleaves!"

Jody was gone, or going.

The camera moved in on the beautiful black girl. She was standing by a grand piano, smiling as the audience gave her a standing welcome. She smiled at her accompanist, waiting. Then, as the applause died, she began. At any other time I would have enjoyed her enormously. One of my favorite singers is Lena Horne, and I have to admit that Sally Cleaves could give the great Lena a run for her money. She chose old standards to sing—"It Was Just One of Those Things," "Old Black Magic," "He's Just My Bill." The audience didn't want to let her go, but it was time for more commercials. Paul Newman made a plea for funds to fight MS. A bunch of kids swarmed around a young mother who served them Kool-Aid.

The Camera came back to the guest platform, where a smiling Sally Cleaves sat with Dick Thomas, Johnny Molloy, and Ross Lubelle. Some chitchat about her career, and then Thomas introduced his next guest.

"One of the most brutal crimes involving an unbelievable number of your friends and neighbors is child abuse. Statistics show that a large percentage of young criminals picked up on our streets today have been the victims of physical abuse by their parents. My next guest is an expert on this important subject. Won't you please welcome Dr. Ralph Snodgrass."

Applause as the bony-faced doctor made his entrance.

"Enough!" Chambrun said in a harsh voice.

There was no need to watch anymore. Jody had been gone from the guest lounge when the doctor had made that entrance the day before. The master reel had shown us zilch, nothing, zero.

Those of us in the control booth sat silent, waiting for Chambrun or Hardy to dictate the next move. Through the glass panel I could see people crowding forward on the stage, looking up at the booth, waiting for instructions like the rest of us. Banazak was there with his two assistants, Picone and Brown. I caught a glimpse of Jake Floyd involved in a conversation with a couple of his musicians. Johnny Molloy, who would be co-hosting today's show, was there. Cameramen, lighting technicians, the whole crew, were waiting for what was to come next. Jerry Dodd, our security chief, was there with Captain Ben Stryker talking his ear off. At least Jerry had managed to keep Stryker from circulating on his own. Everyone seemed to be talking at once, but in the control booth we couldn't hear them.

"One or two questions, Mr. Meador," Chambrun said.

"Shoot," Meador said.

"In making a moving picture film several cameras are at work simultaneously. Each of those cameras films a part of the action. Later on the film editor and the director view the films from all the cameras, choose the shots they want, and splice them together into what becomes the final, the master film. But the out-takes, the shots they don't use, still exist. If they change their minds later, they can go back and insert one or more of those out-takes into the master film."

"Right," Meador said.

"But we don't have that here? The shots you didn't select during the show are gone forever?"

"Right again," Meador said.

"Suppose something goes wrong during the show?" Chambrun asked. "Suppose a guest uses a four-letter word that isn't acceptable? How do you deal with that?"

"I can cut quickly to another shot," Meador said, "or go to a commercial. For the live show we're stuck with whatever I can do to cover. For the master reel that goes to stations across the country for later viewing we can cut the bad moment in the master reel, fill in with music or a shot of the audience from some other filming. In other words, we can cut from the master reel and fill in with something we have in stock from some other master reel from the past. But there are no out-takes from the show itself. The other cameras don't record anything that wasn't selected at the time here in the control booth."

"You don't run over in time and have film to spare?"

Meador gave The Man a thin smile. "We've been doing this show for almost twenty years, Mr. Chambrun. We don't run over. We come out right on the button."

"So what we've seen now is all we're ever going to see?"

"Right."

"Which was nothing," Lieutenant Hardy said.

Chambrun's eyes were very bright in their deep pouches as he glanced at the detective. "Not exactly nothing," he said.

He got up and walked out of the booth.

Those of us who watched him go were gaping a little, I think. None of us had seen anything. What had we missed?

CHAMBRUN HAD given me a little nod of the head as he left the booth, a signal that I was to follow him. He ignored the people onstage and walked briskly out of the ballroom and into the lobby.

The lobby was jammed with new hopefuls there to see today's Dick Thomas Show. We had, literally, to shoulder our way through them to get to the Carnation Room, which had been set aside for the press.

"I promised to check in with them after we'd seen the film," Chambrun managed to tell me.

The ladies and gentlemen of the press were waiting for him, along with photographers and a couple of TV cameramen. In the years that Chambrun had run the Beaumont, through violences and scandals and political activities, he had been dead on the level with the press. They trusted him. He saw that as a necessity, or we would have been swarmed over by eager reporters trying to dig out stories for themselves, prying into places they had no right to be, invading the privacy of hotel guests who had a right to be protected. There was an unspoken agreement between Chambrun and the press. He would never mislead them or lie to them, and they, in turn, would respect his requirements for an unruffled life in the hotel.

A radio news show was going full blast as Chambrun and I walked into the Carnation Room, something about riots in Iran. Someone switched it off the minute they saw Chambrun. A chatter of conversation instantly ended.

"Sorry to have kept you waiting so long," Chambrun said. "We have seen the film of yesterday's Dick Thomas Show up to the point we know that Jody Powers was gone. The result is somewhat disappointing."

"Somewhat?" Eliot Stevens, the man from International, asked. He seemed to have been appointed a spokesman for the whole group. He was a friend from many past stories.

Chambrun explained that he'd hoped there'd be some film from the "out" cameras that would have picked up something. Those cameras didn't record.

"The master reel shows almost nothing," Chambrun said.

"'Almost'?" Stevens asked.

"What it showed," Chambrun said, "is that nothing whatever went wrong with the first thirty-five or forty minutes of the show. Everything went exactly as rehearsed and planned. That is something. Almost nothing, but something."

"We've all had a chance to look at the backstage and the guest lounge," Stevens said. "There is a way to walk from the dressing rooms to the guest lounge without being seen by the audience. But it's wide open, Mr. Chambrun. Anyone working backstage can see people come and go. No one admits to seeing Jody leave the lounge, alone or with someone. It doesn't seem possible."

"It isn't possible," Chambrun said quietly.

"Then someone is lying?"

"Wouldn't you, if you had just killed someone?"

A murmur of voices went around the room. A woman from one of the networks asked the next question. "There has been scuttlebutt to the effect that the disappearance of Victor Lewis almost three years ago and the murder of Ted Valentine yesterday are connected in some way. Will you comment on that, Mr. Chambrun?"

"It's a theory, compounded by a coincidence," Chambrun said. "Both young men removed from the scene on a day Sharon Brand was due to appear on the Dick Thomas Show. It could spell a connection. Jody Powers thought there was one, and she is violently dead. If I had any lingering doubts about a connection, they've been unpleasantly eliminated."

I felt someone tugging at my sleeve and I turned to face Johnny Thacker, the day bell captain. "Get the boss out of there on the double," Johnny said. "More big trouble."

"What are you talking about?" I asked him.

"The cop who was assigned to guard Sharon Brand has been skulled and the lady herself is gone from Fourteen B. There's hell to pay up there, Mark. I don't think the boss would want to let the press in on it just yet."

TWO

CHAMBRUN HAD that hanging judge look on his face as we rode an elevator up to Fourteen. We didn't know any more than what Johnny Thacker had told me except that the alert to locate Chambrun had come from Betsy Ruysdale in his office.

Fourteen was almost as hectic as the lobby. People were crowded outside the door of Suite B. One of Jerry Dodd's men was barring the curious, other guests, the floor maids, a couple of bellhops, from pushing in. Chambrun and I had no trouble passing through into the vestibule.

In the room beyond there were more people crowded around a stretcher on which Sergeant Croft lay, covered with a blanket, his head swathed in bandages. Dr. Partridge, our house physician, was kneeling beside the stretcher. A couple of bellhops were preparing to lift it, I presumed to carry it out and down to the hotel's hospital facilities on the main floor.

Lieutenant Hardy, looking as if he'd been carved out of rock on the face of Mount Rushmore, was talking with Red Baxter, Sharon Brand's agent. Baxter looked pale and angry, and when he saw Chambrun, he spun away from Hardy.

"You didn't wait to ask her if she wanted to be set up," he said. "You just let it happen!" He was in a fury and he was also frightened.

The story came out, partly from Baxter, partly from Hardy. Baxter had called Sharon on the house phone about a quarter to ten, while Chambrun and I had been with Hardy in the ballroom, about to view the master reel of the Thomas Show. It was the earliest time in the morning Baxter had thought it was "decent" to call. The policeman, presumably Sergeant Croft who was on duty again, had answered, and when Baxter identified himself, Sharon had come on the line.

"She sounded fine, perfectly normal," Baxter told us. "I asked her if I could come up to see her and she said it might save her life!" His laugh was bitter. "She was dying from just sitting around—'waiting for something to happen.' Jesus!"

Baxter said it took him about five minutes to finish dressing in his room on the third floor, and then he took an elevator up to Fourteen. He rang the doorbell of Suite B and waited for the cop or Sharon to let him in. Nothing happened. He rang and rang. Why didn't they answer? They were expecting him. He walked down the hall to the housekeeper's room where Mrs. Kniffin, one of our solid people, let him use her house phone to call Suite B. The phone kept ringing but produced no results.

"You scared me about her safety last night," Baxter said to Chambrun. "I was scared all over again. I persuaded your Mrs. Kniffin that something was wrong and she went back down the hall with me, bringing her passkey. She had no trouble opening the door. We walked in and—and found him." He pointed to the stretcher.

"How bad is he?" Chambrun asked Dr. Partridge, who was listening.

"Bad," the doctor said. "Hammered over the head like Valentine was."

"Sharon was nowhere!" Baxter said. "It was less than fifteen minutes after I'd first called and talked to her."

"The service door at the rear is unbolted," Hardy said. "It seems likely she went out that way."

"Was *taken out* that way!" Baxter said.

"Where did you find Croft?" Chambrun asked.

"Almost where he is now," Hardy said. "They moved him just enough to lift him on the stretcher."

"Mrs. Kniffin called the doctor and your high-powered security people—who let this happen!" Baxter said.

"The police were guarding her, not my people," Chambrun said. "Sergeant Croft is a first-class man, isn't he, Hardy?"

"The best," Hardy said.

"The stupid sonofabitch let the killer in, probably thinking he was me. Didn't ask for an ID; just took it for granted," Baxter said.

"I don't believe that," Hardy said.

"But it happened!" Baxter shouted at him. "Whoever slugged your man, Lieutenant, couldn't have gotten in unless your Sergeant Croft let him in."

Chambrun gave the agent a cold look. "Mrs. Kniffin got in with a passkey," he said.

"So anyone who wants can find himself a passkey?" Baxter asked.

"Not easily. Almost impossibly. But someone had a key to this suite."

"Who?" Hardy asked.

"The man who killed Valentine," Chambrun said. "The man who came up here after Valentine was dead, removed all Valentine's clothes, belongings, luggage. He got the key from Valentine's dead body. He still had it this morning."

"Croft was in here, waiting for Baxter to arrive," Hardy said. "The killer let himself noiselessly into the vestibule, slipped up behind Croft and slugged him."

"When will Croft be able to talk?" Chambrun asked the doctor.

"Maybe never," Dr. Partridge said, "unless I get him out of here and down to where I have the proper equipment to deal with him; to get him, at least alive, to a hospital."

"Move him," Hardy said.

The bellhops lifted the stretcher and carried the motionless Croft out toward the elevators, accompanied by the doctor and one of Jerry Dodd's security men.

"Where do we look for Sharon?" Baxter asked. He sounded exhausted from his own emotions.

"We're checking the service elevator, the fire stairs at the back," Hardy said.

"She could have been taken anywhere, up or down," Baxter said.

"But certainly not by way of the front halls or the front elevators," Hardy said. He sounded grim. "You couldn't carry a body out that way. Too many people, lobby swarming with them. She couldn't be walked out with a gun at her back. Everyone in God's world would know her by sight. Those goons in the lobby would be all over her for autographs."

"She's dead, stuffed away in a closet somewhere!" Baxter said, his voice broken.

"I think not," Chambrun said.

"Hunch?" Hardy asked him.

Chambrun shook his head slowly. "If all this man wanted to do was kill her, why take her somewhere else to do it? He slugs Croft and all he has to do is slug Sharon and leave her here to be found. Why try to move her somewhere else for an execution?"

"You think she ran away from him, got away from him while he was dealing with Croft?" Baxter asked.

"I wish I did," Chambrun said, "because if she'd escaped him, she'd be in my office now, screaming bloody murder for me to do something."

"Then what?" Baxter asked.

"If we're close to right about the motive for what has happened, the disappearance two years and seven months ago of Victor Lewis, the murder of Ted Valentine, then Sharon is the person this monster wants to hurt. He has taken her somewhere and left her, alone, I think. When he can he will get back to her and stretch out what he thinks of as her punishment."

"Why risk leaving her alone?" Baxter asked.

"There must be a thousand rooms, closets, storage places to search," Hardy said. "Take us a week unless we got lucky."

"We've got to try to get lucky," Chambrun said.

"I still don't understand why you think he'd left Sharon alone somewhere," Baxter said.

"Because," Chambrun said, "he had only a little time. He had to be somewhere. His absence from where he was supposed to be would point to him."

"You're not making sense," Baxter said.

"I think I am," Chambrun said. "Jody Powers was interested in Claudine Trudeau, a dead girl who, six

years ago, had a connection with the Dick Thomas
Show. Jody was backstage at the Thomas Show when
the killer persuaded her to go to her death. I'm guessing the man we're after is connected with the show, had
to be back in the ballroom for rehearsals for today's
epic, and for the show itself. He won't really be free to
finish with Sharon until the show is over at six o'clock
tonight. We have a chance, gentlemen—if I'm right.''

PEOPLE HAVE BEEN lost in the Beaumont before; a kid
wandering away from his family's rooms, an amnesia
victim, a woman snatched by a sex-nut, a millionaire
industrialist held somewhere inside our world by ex-
tortionist kidnappers. I suppose there could be dozens
of reasons I haven't thought of for someone to disappear. The point of that, long ago, Chambrun along
with Jerry Dodd and other key personnel had set up
routines for an instant search. There are maids on duty
on all forty floors of the Beaumont, bellhops and security people circulating, maintenance people on duty
in the basement areas along with the kitchen people,
management staff in the offices, operators on the telephone switchboard, doormen at the guest entrances on
the avenue and the side streets. Five minutes after an
alert is sounded, no recognizable person could leave the
hotel without being stopped and questioned. It
wouldn't take a week, as Hardy had suggested, to go
over the hotel from roof to subbasement. The routines
were as carefully planned as a fire drill on shipboard.
Guests would be told there was some kind of maintenance problem when someone appeared to search a
room or a suite. If guests were not in, their rooms could
be entered with passkeys.

"Looking for a human being isn't like looking for a missing watch, or ring, or a jewel that's fallen out of a setting. A man or woman is either there or not there," I'd heard Jerry Dodd say.

In Sharon Brand's case no one needed one of those "approximate" descriptions—approximately five feet six, approximately 109 pounds, blond hair, blue eyes, white Caucasian female. Only a celibate monk out of a Tibetan monastery wouldn't know who she was instantly, on sight.

The alarms and alerts were out.

"Barn doors locked a half hour after the horse was stolen," Baxter said bitterly.

"She wasn't carried out dead or unconscious," Chambrun said. "Not in broad daylight on a busy morning with a thousand movie fans swarming the lobby. If she walked out—forced, let us say, by a gun in her ribs—she still would have been noticed by someone on our staff—a doorman, a bellman, one of dozens of extra security people in the lobby. It may not have been reported, but it will be—if it happened— when everyone has been alerted."

"And if it isn't?" Baxter said.

"Then we'll know she's in the hotel and we'll find her," Chambrun said.

"Dead or alive," Baxter said.

Chambrun gave him that frozen look. "Quite right," he said. "Dead or alive."

Sharon Brand had been alive and well at a quarter to ten. That was when Baxter had called her suite and talked, first to Croft and then to her. Everything had been in order then. Invited up, Baxter had taken five minutes—approximately—to dress; another six or seven minutes—approximately—to journey up to Fourteen B. Then there had been the ringing of the doorbell which produced no answer, a trip down the hall to Mrs. Kniffin's quarters where he had tried phoning again. No answer. Then he and Mrs. Kniffin had gone back down the hall where Mrs. Kniffin had used her passkey to let them into the suite. Whatever had happened to Sharon had taken place within a space of twenty minutes—approximately. If Chambrun was right, the killer had walked down the hall on Fourteen, risking being seen by guests, maids, whomever, and let himself into the suite with Ted Valentine's key.

"You don't know that he didn't come in the service door at the rear," Baxter said.

"It was bolted," Hardy said.

"It isn't bolted now," Baxter said.

"Because they went out that way."

"You don't know it was bolted before. You can't know till Sergeant Croft tells you he didn't unbolt it for some reason."

"What reason?" Hardy asked.

Baxter was determined. "He heard someone emptying the trash barrel in the back hall," he said. "He had something he wanted to go and opened the back door to hand it out, forgot to bolt it when he closed the door again."

"Not Croft," Hardy said. "That isn't the kind of thing he would forget."

"In addition to the regular front door lock there's a chain lock," Baxter said. "Shouldn't that have been in place? Croft wouldn't have wanted some maid or handyman to be letting himself in with a passkey before he could check out on them, would he?"

Hardy looked unhappy. "It should have been in place," he said.

"But it wasn't," Baxter said. "It wasn't in place when Mrs. Kniffin let us in. It couldn't have been when the person with Ted Valentine's key let himself in, if that's what happened."

The redheaded agent had a pretty solid argument going his way, I thought. You had to believe that Croft had been careless. It was obvious that Hardy didn't want to believe that. Croft was "the best," he had told us.

Chambrun had listened in silence to all this. I could almost hear the wheels turning in his head.

"I want a head check down in the ballroom," he said. "I want to know who from the Thomas Show wasn't there when we were looking at the master reel. That was when whatever happened here happened." He turned to me. "You know some of the people on the show, Mark—the piano player, the research girl. They may loosen up more to a friend than to a cop or to Jerry Dodd. And tell Lou Feldman I'm going to want to look at the first section of the master reel again. Have someone set up a projector and a screen in my office."

None of us had seen anything helpful on that master reel, but Chambrun had said at the time "not exactly nothing." What, I wondered, had we missed?

I left Chambrun with Hardy and Red Baxter in Fourteen B and went back down to the lobby. There was the same turmoil of Dick Thomas fans. I went around the back way to the ballroom. Jerry Dodd, our security man, was there ahead of me. Chambrun had reached Jerry and he was already with Lou Feldman, trying to work out a head check on who had been present and who missing during the time from nine forty-five till a little after ten. He could write off Tony Meador, the director, and the assistants in the control booth. They had been with us the whole time, along with Dick Thomas and Feldman himself. The rest wasn't going to be quite so simple.

"Everyone on the staff and crew had been told to be present," Feldman said. "But they had no specific jobs to do, no special places to be—like during a rehearsal or a show."

While Feldman talked to us in the wings, a disco singer was rehearsing a number onstage. He had his own back-up musicians, four guitar players and a drummer. Jake Floyd was sitting at his piano with his own six-man group in their places on the permanent bandstand. I slipped away and went over to talk to him.

"Be nice to hear some music with a tune to it," Jake said.

"Talk for a minute?" I asked him.

"Why not? Help me to forget what I'm listening to," he said.

I told him what had happened up in Fourteen B. His cigar rolled from one corner of his mouth to the other. His bright little eyes were narrowed. "This is really getting out of hand, for God sake," he said. "Who's next, I wonder?"

"This morning," I said, "when we were looking at the master reel in the control booth, somebody could have gone up from here to Fourteen."

"You asking me if I saw anyone leave here?"

"Or if you were aware that someone was missing," I said.

He shook his head, rolling the cigar across his mouth again. "You were looking at the master reel in the control booth," he said. "The rest of us were watching it on the monitor out here onstage. We knew the cops and your security people hoped to see something—someone going into the guest lounge where the Powers broad was supposed to be, or maybe Powers leaving the lounge with someone. I was watching the monitor like everyone else. Had no reason to."

"After it was over, anyone missing?"

"Not me, or any of my six guys," Jake said. "I suppose Banazak would know about his people, and the head cameraman might know about his, the lighting man his. They weren't working, you know. There was no place they were supposed to be, so no one was checking. Like me, people were watching the tape, the master, not checking."

"But if you think back, Jake, you might remember not seeing someone you would expect to see?"

"I didn't expect or not expect to see anyone this morning," he said. "Twiggy Sayles called me in my hotel across town. I can't afford to stay here with you." He grinned at me. "I do drink in your saloons. It seemed like I'd just hit the sack when Twiggy called and told me everyone connected with the show was asked to report early—nine-thirty. The cops were going to run yesterday's master reel. There might be questions. Would I call my boys, the band. They were scattered in different hotels, but I reached them all." His cigar rolled. "They're apt to be shacked up God knows where with God knows who, but if they were making out this morning, it was in their own beds."

"And nobody was noticeably missing when they started to show the master reel?"

"It's like I said. I had no reason to check or care," Jake said. "Wish I could help. You know, maybe you'd ought to issue hard hats to everyone. Some crazy guy going around braining people. The cop going to live?"

"They're getting him to a hospital. The house doctor didn't sound too hopeful. He was pretty well battered."

The disco singer had come to the end of his number on stage. Meador, in the control booth, was giving him some last-minute instructions about positioning himself a little differently for the lights and camera.

"Sorry, but I'm involved in the next intro," he said, and faced his piano keyboard.

I went looking for Laura Sayles, the girl with the Twiggy flat chest, who was Dick Thomas's right arm on the show. I found her in the guest lounge, talking to a well-known Las Vegas television comic who was to do a routine and be interviewed on today's show. She was armed with a clipboard, the badge of the trade. She gave me a little signal that was a request to wait.

From where I stood I could see the cameramen on their dollies, ready to move in and out on the scene. If I looked up, I was blinded by lights. We were snowed under by violence and murder, but Dick Thomas's people were in position to carry on as though nothing at all out of the way had happened. The people in the hinterlands weren't to be denied their daily dose of Dick Thomas charm.

The Las Vegas comic took off for the guest lounge to wait for his cue and Twiggy Sayles joined me.

"How awful," she said. "Have they found Miss Brand?"

"They've just started to look," I said. "You know that Chambrun is pretty well convinced we're after someone on your show, Twiggy?"

"I know, and it doesn't make sense," she said. The Dick Thomas show was her life, and Dick Thomas, I suspected, was her dream man.

"Dick, and Tony Meador, and the assistant directors, and Lou Feldman are all in the clear," I told her. "They were all in the control booth with us when someone was upstairs slugging a cop and taking off with Sharon Brand. But we have to check out on everyone else. Even if someone went to the john he's going to have to prove it."

She turned back two or three pages on her clipboard. "I checked people in when they came here this morning to watch the master reel," she said. "It was a double check, because each department head was supposed to check on his people, too. Lou Feldman asked me to double check, and to make sure there wasn't anyone here who shouldn't be. No press. No Thomas fans who might have found a way to sneak in. Not connected with the show were you, Mr. Chambrun, Lieutenant Hardy, your security man." She glanced up from her notes.

"Jerry Dodd," I said.

She made a note. "With him was a man whom he said was Jody Powers's fiancé."

"Ben Stryker, an airline pilot."

"Dodd vouched for him in any case," she said, making another note. "My records show that everyone connected with the show, everyone from Dick down to the gofor who goes for coffee was present. No one missing.''

"But after they checked in they could have left. Someone could have left.''

She gave me a tight little smile. "So ask the police,'' she said.

"The police are asking me to ask you,'' I said.

"Don't be absurd, Mark,'' she said. "Don't you know that Lieutenant Hardy had every possible way into this place covered by a cop? That was to keep unwanted people out. But if anyone left, they'd know, wouldn't they?''

That was a tough one to answer.

"And you're ready to say, positively, that no one from the show was missing, came late?''

"I'm ready to swear it on the Bible in court!'' she said.

I told her Chambrun wanted to look at the master reel again in his office.

"I can supply the tape,'' she said. "He'll have to dig up his own screen and projector.''

WE WEREN'T GOING to be able to keep the Sharon Brand story from breaking very long. Too many people on the Dick Thomas Show were being questioned about it. The so-called ladies and gentlemen of the press in the Carnation Room were going to get wind of it at any moment, and there was going to be hell to pay when they discovered we hadn't kept our promise to let them know when there was anything to tell.

I went back out into the lobby and pushed my way through the logjam of Thomas fans to a house phone.

I called Chambrun's office and found he was back there.

"Surrounded by the enemy," Betsy Ruysdale told me.

"What enemy?"

"Red Baxter, Captain Ben Stryker," Ruysdale said. "Each of them knows a better way to handle things than the boss."

"I need to talk to him."

Chambrun's voice was crisp and impersonal when he came on. He was talking in front of "the enemy."

"Anything turn up?" he asked.

I told him what Twiggy Sayles had told me. All present and accounted for, with Hardy's cops supposed to be able to tell us if anyone left after we'd begun to run the master reel.

"That all?" he asked, without the slightest indication that he'd reacted at all.

"I'm concerned about the press," I said. "The minute anyone walks out of that rehearsal in the ballroom, the news is going to spread like a brush fire."

"I have visitors here who aren't going to sit on it either," Chambrun said. "I guess it's your job to run with the ball, Mark."

"Now?"

"Now," Chambrun said, and hung up.

I took a deep breath and headed across the lobby to the Carnation Room. The boys and girls were all there with their photographers and TV cameras.

"We were about to send out a search party for you, brother," Eliot Stevens said. "How long do you think we can sit here twiddling our thumbs? You promised—"

"I have a new story for you," I said.

"We don't want a new story, Mark. We want answers to the old one."

"A close relative," I said. "The cop who was guarding Sharon Brand has been slugged and Miss Brand has disappeared from her suite."

Bedlam. People on the fringes rushing for phones without waiting to hear the whole thing. Cameras clicking, the TV monsters whirring. I was to be the star of this scene.

I gave them the facts, not the theories. Sharon had talked with her agent on the phone at nine forty-five. The cop, Sergeant Croft, had also talked with Baxter then. Twenty minutes later no one responded to the doorbell or the telephone, and Baxter, with the aid of Mrs. Kniffin, had entered the suite and found Croft near death and Sharon gone.

Questions fell on me like hailstones. How was it possible? Eliot Stevens knew Sergeant Croft. He wasn't a careless cop. It was about as possible for her to be taken out of the hotel unrecognized as it would to have removed President Carter.

Since yesterday morning, I told them, when Jody Powers came plummeting down the service elevator shaft, every entrance-exit to and from the hotel had been covered by police or by our own security people. In the twenty-minute period of time in which Sharon had to have been abducted that security had been tight as a drum. There was no doubt in Chambrun's mind, or Hardy's for the matter, that Sharon was still somewhere in the hotel. There were routine procedures for top-to-bottom search, and they were already in operation.

"Do the police think it's kidnapping?" a woman reporter asked.

"If it is, there haven't been any ransom demands I've heard of," I said.

"Who would be likely to receive such a demand?" the woman persisted. "Miss Brand has no family that I've ever heard of; the current man in her life was murdered yesterday. Who would kidnappers approach? Her lawyer, her banker, her agent?"

"Ray Baxter, her agent, is floating around the hotel," I said. "He's the person to answer that question for you." I didn't tell the lady that neither Chambrun nor Hardy or any of us in the know believed this was a routine kidnapping with a ransom demand to be forthcoming. What Chambrun feared was a lot grimmer than that—some kind of psycho out to terrorize Sharon Brand. She might be tortured and killed, that unforgettable face mutilated. God knows what! A demand for money, even in telephone numbers, could be easily met. Sharon Brand was floating in money. The entire film industry would have chipped in to provide a queen's ransom if necessary. I knew Chambrun hadn't considered anything that simple was in the offing. But the lady reporter's suggestion provided me with an out.

"You can all see how touchy the situation is," I told them all. "If there gets to be a negotiation with a kidnapper, we aren't going to be able to inform you until a deal is made and Sharon Brand has been safely returned."

"But you say there hasn't been a demand?" Eliot Stevens said.

"Not that I know of. But there hasn't been much time, Eliot. If they got her out of the hotel, which seems unlikely, they would have to hide her somewhere before they could start dealing."

"And if they didn't get her out of the hotel?"

"We'll find her," I said. "In time we'll find her."

"It's pretty obvious that Chambrun and Hardy thought the lady was in danger, or why a policeman to guard her?" Eliot said. "It's also obvious they have been thinking Ted Valentine's murderer had some connection with the Dick Thomas Show."

"I think I can tell you this much," I said. "During the twenty to twenty-five minutes from the time when Sharon Brand talked to Red Baxter on the phone and was safe, and Croft was safe, and when we found Croft unconscious and Sharon gone, everyone directly connected with the Dick Thomas Show is accounted for."

"So Chambrun and Hardy had had to change their thinking," Eliot said. "Where does that take them?"

"I honestly don't know," I said. "And now, if you'll excuse me—"

I wasn't hiding anything from them. I didn't know anything to hide. Out in the lobby I ran into Johnny Thacker, the day bell captain. The alarm was out. A floor-by-floor, room-by-room, closet-by-closet search of the Beaumont was underway.

"Anyone but that famous lady could have mingled with this crowd of goons," Thacker said, gesturing toward the noisy Dick Thomas fans, "and slipped out. But that kind of famous face, a celebrity, is exactly what they're all looking for. No way she could have been taken out through this lobby unnoticed. The doormen all know her. She couldn't just walk out onto the street. They all say, flatly, she didn't."

"How long will the preliminary search take?" I asked him. He'd been drilled in the routine.

"You can't hide a grown woman under a rug or in a bureau drawer," he said. "I should think in less than an hour we should find her—if she's here."

"If she couldn't be taken out, she's here," I said.

Thacker gave me a twisted little smile. "Parachute off the roof," he said.

No way, and yet there might be a way none of us had considered for the moment.

Up in Chambrun's office someone had already provided a movie screen and a projector. The Man was there with Hardy, Red Baxter still hanging to their coattails. Jerry Dodd, Ruysdale told me, was supervising the search of the hotel. A young man I didn't know was at the projector, ready to run the master reel of yesterday's Dick Thomas Show. Baxter was fuming.

"This is a sinful waste of time," he said. "I know what happened to the Powers girl is important in the long run, but looking at what happened yesterday isn't going to get us any closer to what's happened to Sharon."

"Maybe not, maybe," Chambrun said. "If you'll draw the curtains, Ruysdale."

As the room was darkened, Baxter went on protesting. The truth was each of us had a different stake in this game. Hardy had a job—solving homicides. He probably placed no greater importance on any one of them—Ted Valentine, Jody Powers, and now, possibly, Sharon Brand. Emotionally, Jody Powers was my chief concern. Baxter had no one on his mind except Sharon. And Chambrun? I think his main concern was to punish the person who had upset the orderly operation of the hotel. He cared for Sharon, I think, but he cared more for the Beaumont.

Chambrun had moved around from behind his desk to the young man at the projector.

"I understand there is a chart of the show that tells exactly how much time each segment took," he said.

The young man referred to his clipboard. "In theory there are four commercial breaks in each half hour," he said. "So that each segment runs about six minutes. Twenty-four minutes of show, six minutes of commercials."

"Quite a price to pay for free entertainment," Chambrun said. "Six minutes in each half hour being convinced that you need a breath freshener."

"It varies a little, depending on the importance of the guest," the young man said. "One half hour may have only four minutes of commercials, the next eight."

"I'm only interested in the tape through the Sally Cleaves bit," Chambrun said. "After that we know Miss Powers was gone from the guest lounge. You have a stopwatch, Ruysdale?"

"I have," Miss Ruysdale said.

"Time each performing segment and each commercial segment, please. You can start the tape, Mr. Carey," Chambrun said to the young man.

We had all seen it before: the shot of the exterior of the Beaumont, the announcement from the announcer, the entrance of Dick Thomas and his rendition of "I Get No Kick from Champagne." There was the thunder of applause, and Dick Thomas with his *"We'll be back in a moment."*

"Hold it," Chambrun said.

The tape stopped running, Dick Thomas frozen in the picture with his mouth open.

"Three and a half minutes," Ruysdale said.

"Time the commercials, please. Okay, Mr. Carey."

The tape started again. There were two commercials.

"Two minutes," Ruysdale said.

"The commercials will be all exactly two minutes," Carey said. "They're filmed in advance, spliced in."

We went on that way, through the introduction of Johnny Molloy and his brilliant song-and-dance routine to "Top Hap, White Tie, and Tails." There were two shots along the way of Jake Floyd and his musicians. Then two minutes of commercials and the tape picked up with Molloy on the interview stand with Thomas.

"There is nothing recorded that shows Molloy going to that chair on the interview stand?" Chambrun asked. "Or anyone else changing positions?"

"He was seen by the audience, of course," Carey said. "But it's not recorded on the master reel."

"Two minutes of repositioning that we never see," Chambrun said.

"That's how it is," young Mr. Carey said.

The tape started again and went on with the Molloy interview. Three minutes of that, and then a commercial. Once more Chambrun ordered the tape stopped after the *"We'll be back in a moment"* cue. There had been three and a half minutes of song and dance, three minutes of interview, four minutes of commercials. Ten and a half minutes in and around Johnny Molloy.

"Not too much time devoted to a big-name star like Molloy," Chambrun said.

"He's the co-host for the whole week," Carey said. "He's in with Dick on most of the interviews, and he has another song and dance at the end of each show. Plenty of exposure, Mr. Chambrun."

"Keep going," Chambrun said.

So it went, through the interview with Ross Lubelle, the *Dracula* man, and the commercials surrounding him. Chambrun stopped the tape again and spoke to all of us.

"During the time used by the commercials that follow this interview with Lubelle, we come to the critical moment, as far as Jody Powers was concerned. Sally Cleaves, the singer, is in the guest lounge with Jody. Am I right in supposing, Mr. Carey, that during the two minutes of commercials following the Lubelle interview the stage manager or one of his assistants would notify Miss Cleaves that it was time to position herself for her entrance?"

"Correct," Carey said.

"It was the one named Wally Brown yesterday," I reminded Chambrun.

I was not applauded for my help.

"Two minutes of commercials," Chambrun said. "Sally Cleaves moves out of the guest lounge with Jody Powers still there, left behind. Start the tape again, Mr. Carey."

The tape began running and we got the two minutes of commercials. Then the camera was on Dick Thomas while he announced his next guest. The curtains at center stage opened and the camera moved in on Sally Cleaves, standing by the piano, smiling at her accompanist, a round-faced black man. Jake Floyd's musicians sat motionless in the background. Applause, applause. The pianist began his intro music and the camera went back to Sally Cleaves and her marvelous rendition of "It Was Just One of Those Things." Applause. Another cut to the accompanist and a new intro, and then back to Sally Cleaves and "Old Black Magic." She was so damn good I wished I could listen to her without other things on my mind. More applause, another cut to the accompanist, and then Sally Cleaves went into "He's Just My Bill."

"Keep it rolling, Mr. Carey," Chambrun said.

There was thunderous applause, a shot of the audience on their feet clapping and shrieking as Dick Thomas joined the singer at center stage, also applauding.

"We'll be back in a moment."

Two minutes of commercials, and then the camera picked up Dick Thomas and Sally Cleaves on the interview stand, flanked by Johnny Molloy and Ross Lubelle. Then a close-up of Thomas.

"One of the most brutal crimes involving an unbelievable number of your friends and neighbors is child abuse. Statistics show that a large percentage of young criminals picked up on our streets today have been the victims of physical abuse by their parents. My next guest is an expert on this important subject. Won't you please welcome Dr. Ralph Snodgrass."

The camera cut to center stage again. There was a glimpse of Jake Floyd and his boys playing something to cover the bony doctor. The curtains parted, and then

Snodgrass appeared and started toward the interview stand.

"Cut," Chambrun said. "Times, please, Ruysdale—beginning with the commercials following the Ross Lubelle interview."

Ruysdale was ready for him. "Two minutes of commercials," she said. "Introduction of Sally Cleaves and the singing of three songs, nine minutes. Two minutes of commercials. Thirteen minutes in all."

Chambrun glanced at a scowling Hardy. "You saw it, Lieutenant. He had thirteen minutes in which to get Jody out of the guest lounge, into the service elevator, take her up to the eleventh floor and push her down the shaft, and get back to the show and into his proper place, unnoticed. It could be done in thirteen minutes without too much difficulty, wouldn't you say?"

"And stop on the way for a short beer," Hardy said, his voice grim. "But which 'he'?"

"It seems fairly obvious that we should begin with the man we know had nothing to do for thirteen minutes," Chambrun said.

"Nobody on the show has nothing to do for thirteen minutes at any time, Mr. Chambrun," young Mr. Carey said.

"I have to disagree with you," Chambrun said. "It's recorded there on the master reel. You all saw it."

"The tape shows somebody doing nothing for thirteen minutes?" Hardy said.

"It doesn't show him doing nothing," Chambrun said. "But it shows that he had nothing to do connected with the show."

"Double-talk!" Ray Baxter exploded. The agent had kept himself in check for quite a while.

Chambrun glanced at me. "I don't think we have to run the film again for me to make my point. Everyone here but Mr. Baxter and Ruysdale has seen it at least twice. I'm talking about your friend Jake Floyd, Mark."

"Jake!"

"Ross Lubelle's interview ends with a flourish from Jake Floyd's band," Chambrun said. "Now we have two minutes of pre-recorded commercials. In that time Jake Floyd relinquishes his place at the piano to Sally Cleaves' accompanist."

"Terry Tyler," Carey said.

"The next shot we have of the live show is Dick Thomas introducing Miss Cleaves. Then we see Miss Cleaves smiling at the man at the piano, Terry Tyler if that's his name. For the next nine minutes we are reminded twice more by the camera that Terry Tyler is at the piano, not Jake Floyd. Nine minutes of that, then two more minutes of commercials. When Dr. Snodgrass is introduced, we finally see Jake Floyd back at the piano. Thirteen minutes plus, nearly fourteen minutes. Unaccounted for, so far."

"Surely you don't think that Jake Floyd—" I began.

"I want to know what he was doing, or at least what he saw during fourteen minutes when he wasn't occupied by the show."

"The other musicians didn't leave the stand," Hardy said. "There are several shots of them."

"But Jake Floyd left the piano, was out of sight of any camera shots we have," Chambrun said. "We know that because Terry Tyler played for Sally Cleaves. That's recorded on the tape."

"I know Jake," I said. "I just can't believe that he—"

"Surely you must agree that a little conversation with him is called for," Chambrun said.

THREE

I SUPPOSE it's an old cliché—it can't happen to me or to my friends. You read or hear about a violence, a terrible accident, a fire or flood, and you're instinctively certain that nothing like that can happen to you or people you know. It could only happen to some faceless "other guy." Ted Valentine and Victor Lewis were those "other guys" you read about in the paper, but Jody Powers had been a lady I cared for, and Sharon Brand was at least someone I knew—that the whole world knew, for that matter. Now Jake Floyd, a sort of friend, whose talent I respected, who had made me laugh, was under the gun. Murder? Not Jake, I insisted to myself. I knew him. It couldn't be.

Chambrun had, however, made a point I couldn't duck. It was logical in an investigation like this to ask Jake where he'd been and what he'd been doing during those critical fourteen minutes.

Hardy had sent a cop to drag Jake out of the rehearsals in the ballroom. While we waited, Red Baxter kept demanding that we stop playing puzzle games and concentrate on what was the central issue to him. Where was Sharon Brand? Every minute we delayed in finding her could make it too late for her.

"There is a room-to-room search going on, Mr. Baxter," Chambrun told him. "It is something my people are thoroughly trained to do. We should begin to get reports on it presently. Lieutenant Hardy has put

out a general alarm for her in the city, in case by some
fluke she was gotten out of the hotel without being
seen. Meanwhile, you have to understand that I'm
thoroughly convinced that the same person is responsible for the disappearance of Victor Lewis almost three
years ago, the murders of Ted Valentine and Jody
Powers yesterday, and the attack on Sergeant Croft and
the abduction of Sharon today. We think that person
has some connection with Dick Thomas. It doesn't
matter which case we unravel first, we'll have our man
when we do. Right now the Powers case seems to offer
us the best chance. It may show us our quickest way to
locate Sharon."

It wasn't arguable.

Jake Floyd, cigar jutting aggressively out of the
corner of his mouth, was an angry man when Hardy's
detective delivered him to Chambrun's office.

"You better have a damn good reason for this, cop-
per," he said to Hardy. "I'm needed downstairs.
That's my job, my bread and butter."

"Talking to you is mine," Hardy said.

Jake looked past me as though I wasn't there, a
stranger. I guess he saw me as part of an enemy army.
I couldn't blame him. He didn't look surprised when
it was Chambrun, not the Lieutenant, who opened fire
on him.

"We've been looking at the tape of yesterday's show,
Mr. Floyd," Chambrun said.

"I know. I was there," Jake said.

"Again," Chambrun said, indicating the screen and
the projector. "I need an accounting of a certain time
for you."

"What the hell are you talking about? I got nothing to account for," Jake said.

Chambrun sometimes has a very quiet, patient manner. To the sucker who doesn't know him, it's reassuring. To me, knowing him so well, it is a signal that he's out for the kill. He explained to Jake, in that quiet, patient way, that the tape, the master reel, had been a disappointment to us. It didn't show any change of stage positions or camera placements during the commercial breaks. From our view it cut away from people in one place and picked them up, after the home audience had been persuaded to change toothpastes or shaving cream, in another. Everyone had a job in those gaps, and according to Tony Meador, the director, everyone did those jobs.

"Meador, I believe, was telling us the truth—as far as he knew it. But he overlooked someone who had no job for a stretch of nearly fourteen minutes."

That didn't seem to register with Jake.

"In that fourteen-minute span someone persuaded Jody Powers to leave the guest lounge, go onto the service elevator, allow herself to be taken up to the eleventh floor and be pushed down the elevator shaft." If Chambrun expected Jake to show some sign of guilt or anxiety, he was disappointed. "The person who had no job in that fourteen-minute stretch could have been the murderer."

"I don't know anyone that didn't have a job once the show started," Jake said. "Everyone has something to do, right through the show."

"Except you, Mr. Floyd," Chambrun said. He leaned back in his desk chair and took a deep drag on his cigarette, his eyes narrowed against the smoke he exhaled as he watched Jake.

Jake's cigar rolled across his mouth. "You sonofa-bitch," he said, and he charged at Chambrun, intending to lunge over the desk at him.

I don't think of Hardy as being nimble, but he was quick as hell in that instant. He grabbed Jake and literally lifted him back from the desk, like someone picking up a small child. Chambrun hadn't changed his position by an inch.

"I'm not accusing you of anything yet, Mr. Floyd," he said, still quiet and patient. "You didn't play for Sally Cleaves's segment of the show. She had her own man at the piano. There was a gap of fourteen minutes while two sets of commercials were run and the Cleaves girl sang her numbers. You had nothing to do, no responsibility, for that fourteen-minute piece of the show."

Jake shook himself loose from Hardy's grip, but he made no further move toward Chambrun.

"And I'm supposed to have dragged that Powers broad upstairs and heaved her down the elevator shaft?" he asked, his voice shaken.

"You're supposed to tell us how you occupied yourself for that fourteen minutes," Chambrun said. "You knew they were coming up. You knew you were free for that time to do anything you had in mind."

"And you cops and masterminds have gotta find a fall guy," Jake said.

"You are the one person absent from his regular post on the show during that fourteen minutes," Chambrun said. "Meador forgot that you weren't supposed to be at the piano. Everyone who had a job to do did it. But the piano player, in that fourteen minutes, was Terry Tyler, not Jake Floyd.''

"That happens a lot of times in the course of a year," Jake said. "We have singers who come on who have their own musical back-ups—piano players, maybe a whole group. In this case Sally Cleaves just had her own piano player. When the commercial that came on ahead of her started, I left the piano so Tyler could get set.''

"And went where, did what?" Chambrun asked.

"Would you believe a cup of coffee? No, I suppose you wouldn't," Jake said. He was still burning. "There's a coffee machine just off the backstage area outside the dressing rooms. I went there for a cup of coffee. Does that make me a murderer?''

"Who saw you?"

"I don't know if anyone saw me actually getting coffee," Jake said. "The show was on. Everyone paying attention to his particular job. Like you said, I had some free time. One of the stage managers might have seen me leave the backstage.''

"Where is this coffee machine in relation to the guest lounge?" Chambrun asked.

"Other side of the stage," Jake said.

"You didn't have to pass the rear entrance to the lounge to get the coffee?''

"No."

"Could you have seen anyone coming or going to or from that rear entrance to the lounge?''

"I could have if I'd been looking. I wasn't looking.''

"You timed yourself?"

"Hell, man, I could hear Sally singing. I knew when she went into her third number—her 'Bill' number—it was time for me to wander back and take over from Tyler."

"When you started 'wandering' back, did you see anything out of order?"

"That screwball child-abuse doctor was feeling his way around like a blind man. Wally Brown had to grab him and guide him into the lounge to keep him from stumbling right onstage."

"So you saw the lounge then?"

"I was headed back toward it then."

"And you'd spent some twelve or thirteen minutes drinking coffee?"

"Relaxing, for God sake," Jake said. "I had a big show still ahead of me; another routine for Johnny Molloy. Complicated stuff."

"You didn't see anyone backstage who didn't belong there?"

"Not then," Jake said. "Just before the show started I saw Ted Banazak taking the Powers girl and Mark, here, into the lounge. I remember giving you a hello, Mark."

I remembered, too.

"So are you going to take me to the slammer, or do I go back to work?" Jake demanded, his cigar pointed at Chambrun.

Chambrun and Hardy exchanged glances.

"Talk to you after the rehearsal," Hardy said.

"Do I get a chance to find someone who can back up what I told you?" Jake said.

"Don't worry, Mr. Floyd, if there is someone, we'll find him."

We watched Jake almost charge out of the office.

"If no one saw him at the coffee machine—" Hardy muttered.

"If no one saw him, it still could be so," Chambrun said. "If he's a killer, Lieutenant, he's as good an actor as he is a piano player."

The little red button blinked on Chambrun's telephone. He picked up the phone. Calls to him are screened by the switchboard or by Ruysdale.

"Chambrun here," he said. And then he almost jumped out of his chair. He reached down and turned on the squawk box. "Of course, put her through!"

What came out of the box was a kind of broken stage whisper. "For God sake, Pierre, I need help."

You could never mistake that voice, even in a whisper. It was Sharon Brand.

"Where are you, Sharon?"

"God knows—way uptown somewhere—162nd Street. Corner drugstore. I—I think I can see Yankee Stadium not far away."

"What are you doing there—how did you get there?"

Her voice sounded stronger. "How is Sergeant Croft?"

"Emergency care," Chambrun said.

"Did he tell you what happened?"

"He didn't tell anybody anything. He may never tell anybody anything."

"Oh my God!"

"You tell me what happened—and quick!" Chambrun said.

"A man—a man was suddenly in the suite at the hotel. He—he knocked out Sergeant Croft and grabbed me. He had—I don't know what you call it—a stocking mask over his head. I—I never saw his face."

"Go on, Sharon."

"He forced me out the back way, down the service elevator, into a waiting car. He drove me up here—somewhere. I couldn't see where we were driving because he forced me down onto the floor of the car. Then—then we stopped in a back alley sort of place. He dragged me out of the car into a falling-down kind of building. I was—was tied to a chair. He demanded to know how he could reach Red Baxter. Ransom, he said. He was going to demand ransom. I told him—the Beaumont."

"I'm here, love!" Baxter shouted into the squawk box.

"Oh, Red! Oh my God!" she said.

"How did you get where you are?" Chambrun said.

"He left. No phone in the place where he had me—to call you, Red. I—I guess he hadn't tied me too well and I was able to get myself free. I ran. Oh God, Pierre, I ran and ran. This drugstore was the first place that looked as if it might have a phone."

Hardy took over from Chambrun. "This is Lieutenant Hardy, Miss Brand. Listen carefully, and do exactly what I tell you. Call the store manager, or someone working there, and get them to the phone. Then stay out of sight. Your kidnapper may be looking for you, checking from building to building. Minutes after I talk to the store manager and get the address, there'll be a patrol car there with two police officers who'll bring you directly here. Quickly please, Miss Brand, the manager!"

We could hear her move away. In the background there was some kind of music, the sharp jangle of a cash register. It seemed to take forever for someone to get back to us. Evidently the manager took some persuading.

Hardy got an address from him, ordered him to take Miss Brand into a back room and keep her safely there until the patrol car arrived.

"Is she really Sharon Brand?" the manager asked.

"She is really Sharon Brand," Hardy said, "and you'll be in big trouble if anything happens to her before my men get there."

Red Baxter pushed Hardy away from the box. "I'm Miss Brand's manager," he said. "You keep her safe and I promise you you'll be richer before the day's over."

"Will do," the voice said. And that was that.

Chambrun sank back into his desk chair. Hardy was on the phone to a police dispatcher. There would be a patrol car within a block or two of the uptown drugstore. They'd reach Sharon in short order.

"Thank God!" Baxter said. "She sounded all right, don't you think?"

Chambrun's mouth was twisted in a bitter little smile. "Right out of an old Warner Brothers B movie," he said.

RUYSDALE AND I WERE left to notify Jerry Dodd and the staff that the search of the hotel was off. Sharon had been found. Jerry was ordered to hotfoot it up to Fourteen B where Chambrun and Hardy would be expecting him.

My next instructions took me to the Carnation
Room. There I told Eliot Stevens and the other reporters that Sharon had been in touch, she was safe, the
police would be bringing her back to the hotel in a
while. When Hardy was through with her, perhaps she
would be willing to let them talk to her.

Where was she? Where had she been?

Chambrun had instructed me to give them the whole
story. "Half of them will hotfoot it uptown to that
drugstore. The fewer, the merrier for us, Mark."

He'd been right. No sooner had I told the story, giving out the address of the drugstore, than there was an
exodus that almost emptied the room. Eliot Stevens
and three or four others still had me hemmed in.

"So she was kidnapped," Eliot said. "There is no
connection between this and your murders?"

"She is a famous lady, a very rich lady," I said.
"Everyone in New York who reads the papers or lis-
tens to radio and TV knew she was in New York, staying here at the Beaumont, preparing to go on the Dick
Thomas Show. It could have been planned well in advance of the other things that have happened. The
kidnapper wasn't going to let a couple of murders interfere with his scheme."

"Does Chambrun think that?" Eliot asked me.

"He told me to 'turn the mice loose,' which means
let you have the facts," I said.

"Where is he now?" Eliot asked. He wasn't satisfied.

"The police are checking out the fourteenth floor,"
I said. "He's with them, with our security people. They
may get some lead to this creep. And don't try to go up
there, Eliot. You'll be stopped."

"How much can happen to one lady in twenty-four hours?" Eliot wondered. "Her boyfriend gets clubbed to death; a gossip columnist who was her friend gets shoved down an elevator shaft; she gets herself kidnapped. That's rather a lot to take on."

"Which I hope will induce you to show some patience and compassion when the time comes to talk to her," I said.

"I suspect she's a pretty gutsy old girl," Eliot said.

"For God sake, don't use the word 'old' in front of her," I said.

If Sharon Brand had walked in the front door of Fourteen B about then, it wouldn't have been a cozy homecoming. The suite was swarming with plainclothes cops and Jerry Dodd and some of his people.

Chambrun was standing by the mantel, under the Grant Wood painting. I imagined he was trying to visualize the morning scene there: a man in a stocking mask slipping up behind Sergeant Croft and clubbing him before Sharon could scream a warning—if she'd been in the room. Sharon hassled out of the back door, down the elevator, out a basement exit to a waiting car.

"At between nine forty-five and ten in the morning," Chambrun said, evidently reading my mind, "with people up and around, doing their jobs, fresh and alive, not tired from a frazzling day; guests circulating; kitchen crew at full complement; maintenance men at their jobs in the basement. *And every exit covered by a cop or one of Jerry's men.*"

"Someone obviously stepped away for a moment," I said.

"When your job is not to step away, you don't step away," Chambrun said.

"The *Titanic* couldn't be sunk," I said. That was a kind of cliché phrase we used around the hotel. You make sure that certain things can't happen, and then they happen. We called those events "Titanic." They happen too frequently I regret to say.

Right then we were confronted with another Titanic that Hardy and his cops and Jerry Dodd and his security men didn't want to accept. Sergeant Croft was a professional. He had been sent to guard Sharon Brand. He was the last person in the world to be careless about locks, the last person to be caught off base. But he had been, and he might be going to pay for it with his life.

A uniformed cop came in from the vestibule and walked over to Chambrun. "There's a couple out in the front corridor who say it's urgent for them to talk to you, Mr. Chambrun."

"Who are they?"

"Girl's name is Armin. She says she was Jody Powers' secretary. The man is an airline pilot named Stryker. They say they know something that might help—about the Powers case."

Chambrun glanced at me and we followed the cop out through the vestibule and into the front corridor. Nancy Armin was there, peering at us through her big round glasses, vanity forgotten. She was hanging onto Ben Stryker's arm as though she might be blown away if she let go of him.

"Thank you for coming out, Mr. Chambrun," Nancy said in her small, uncertain voice.

"It's about the thing I told you," Stryker said to me.

"What thing?"

The itinerary of the Dick Thomas Show they found in Claudine Trudeau's belongings after she drowned herself."

"Six years ago!" I said.

"Ben told me about it," Nancy said. "We had nothing to do but wait and wait, hoping there'd be some word from the police and Mr. Chambrun, about who—who might have—Jody, I mean."

"So?" Chambrun said.

"You can't just sit and wait!" Nancy said. "I started to go through records and old clippings, hoping I might build up more of a history on Claudine Trudeau than was in Jody's file on her. I—I came across something."

"There's a kind of a bible on film put out every year," Stryker said. "It lists every film made, big or small, with a list of everyone connected with it—cast, director, writers, cameramen, costumers, the works. The only film we knew of that Claudine Trudeau made was the *Beach Boy* epic back in 1971. That was when Rex Hilliard had first brought her to Hollywood."

"The person who directed that film was Tony Meador," Nancy said, "who also directs the Dick Thomas Show."

The missing link, I thought. Hardy had asked everyone on the Thomas Show if they had any knowledge of the Trudeau girl, hoping to explain why Jody had her file out. Meador had certainly kept his mouth shut about having once worked with her.

"He hasn't admitted it now," Stryker said. "He didn't admit knowing her when the Los Angeles police asked questions at the time of her suicide. If Jody had caught up with him, then he may damn well be the one who—"

"If you're thinking of making Meador a personal cause, forget it," Chambrun said.

"But he lied, kept it to himself!" Stryker said. "He knew about Claudine Trudeau six years ago, and he knew about her when you started asking about her yesterday—today."

"But he didn't kill Jody Powers," Chambrun said. "Jody was alive, with Mark in the guest lounge, when yesterday's show began. She was seen, alive, by three different people in the guest lounge after the show started. That is about forty minutes. Meador was in the control booth from the time the show began until it ended—never left his post. He and his three assistants, along with Dick Thomas and Johnny Molloy, are the six people on the show who have absolutely airtight alibis for the time Jody was lured away and killed. Interesting that he didn't tell us that he knew Claudine Trudeau, but he didn't kill Jody."

"You'll question him?" Stryker asked.

"Of course. But don't sharpen your knife for him, Captain Stryker. He's not your man."

FOUR

THE REHEARSAL for that day's Dick Thomas Show was just about over when one of Hardy's men hauled Tony Meador out of the control booth and brought him up to Fourteen B. I honestly don't think he guessed what was coming. I think he expected more questions about the master reel. Hardy, Chambrun and I, an observer, talked to him in the suite's kitchenette. Hardy's people were still involved in an inch-by-inch search of the living room, hoping for some clue to Sharon's stocking-masked abductor.

"You directed a film called *The Boys on the Beach* back in 1971," Chambrun said.

Meador's thin, dark face hardened. "So that's it," he said.

"That's it, Mr. Meador," Chambrun said.

Meador reached for a cigarette and lit it. His hands weren't quite steady. "Yes, I knew Claudine Trudeau," he said.

"And lied about it to the Los Angeles police six years ago, and to us yesterday," Hardy said.

"Because I didn't know anything that would help," Meador said. "She was cast in that film, nine years ago. Casting director's choice, not mine. She was Rex Hilliard's protégée, and Rex had pull at the studio."

"So you directed her in that film. You got to know her afterwards?"

"Not what I think you mean," Meador said. "She was Hilliard's property, living with him."

"Let me get something straight," Chambrun said. "You told us you'd been directing the Dick Thomas Show for what—eighteen, twenty years? How come this film, nine years ago?"

"Summer break, time off," Meador said. "I got the offer to do *Beach Boys* and I took it. It was a quickie, and it was a dog."

"But you got to know her during the filming," Hardy said.

Meador gave us a wry smile. "I had to get to know her. She was so lousy! I couldn't fire her. She was Rex Hilliard's doll. I had to try to get something out of her by playing kindly old Uncle Tony, pushing her along step by step, gesture by gesture. She couldn't speak a line without making you cover your ears. I tried to make what I could, photographically, out of her extraordinarily beautiful body. I offered up a silent prayer of thanksgiving when it was over. She was a total nothing as an actress."

"So what came next?" Hardy asked.

"Blessed relief from working with kids who were all ambition and no talent," Meador said. "Someone has said that's what the streets of Hollywood are paved with—ambitious kids who couldn't make it. There's only one Sharon Brand in a generation. They tell me she's safe."

"We're about to see," Chambrun said. "Your particular no-talent wound up feeding the fishes in the Pacific Ocean, Meador. The police questioned you and the rest of the Dick Thomas staff about her at the time of her suicide. You lied to them?"

"You obviously haven't checked with the Los Angeles cops or you'd know I didn't," Meador said. He took a drag on his cigarette. "I told them I knew her, had worked with her in one film, had seen her 'around,' part of an army of eager, hopeless kids. Yes, I knew the story about Rex Hilliard and that Hilliard had left her for greener grass, more glitter, more glamor. Did I know anything about any family, any current boyfriend, someone probably working for Dick Thomas? They had this itinerary they'd found in her room. Now that itinerary is a mimeographed sheet turned out by Dick Thomas's people, handed to all of us who work for him, available to anyone on the outside who asks for it. I didn't know anything about her family, or any current boyfriend who might be working on the Dick Thomas Show. But if I'd told them I knew how she got the itinerary, I would have been tagged for it. And I wasn't it. Never close, never wanted to be close. I was just kindly old 'Uncle Tony.'"

"We're running out of time, Mr. Meador," Chambrun said. "Sharon Brand will be arriving here any moment." He hinted at a smile. "She'll take the stage from you, from all of us."

"Claudine Trudeau had no family. As a baby, she was, dramatically enough, left in a basket on the steps of an orphanage. She had no name, no identity. She grew up in an institution. A couple of foster homes didn't work. When she was fifteen, she took off on her own. I suppose the authorities tried, perfunctorily, to find her. But there was no one who cared. Shopgirl, waitress, carhop and, I suspect, a little paid sex along the way. She wound up as an apprentice in a stock company in 1970. There she met Hilliard, dazzled him with her sexual talents, and persuaded him to take her to Hollywood. She invented a name, a family, French origins. All fake. As long as he stayed with her, it didn't matter that she had no talent, no gifts of any sort. He left her for Sharon Brand. Before that I'd had my experience with her in *The Boys on the Beach*. I was kindly old Uncle Tony. One day in 1974 Claudine came to see me. She was hysterical, perhaps, I thought, suicidal. Hilliard had left her for Sharon Brand. Without his support she couldn't even get modeling jobs. End of the line for her. I spent as much time as I could trying to persuade her to forget about being an actress; it would bring her nothing but disappointment and grief. She was desperate; no friends, no one to turn to, no lover who loved! I finally thought I'd persuaded her to, at least, face the next day. I wasn't going to be around to help. The Thomas Show was taking off, but if she needed help she could try reaching me and I'd do what I could. I gave her a mimeographed copy of the Thomas itinerary." Meador crushed out his cigarette in a saucer on the table. "End of report. Three or four days later she was dead. She never tried to reach me."

"But you didn't tell the police you'd given her the itinerary?" Hardy asked.

"Listen, Lieutenant, I work for Dick Thomas. He is Mr. Nice Guy, Mr. Family Man, Mr. Puritan Morals. If he knew that I was involved with a little tramp who had staged a scandalous scene with an important Hollywood lady before she drowned herself, it might have cost me my job. All the wrong conclusions would have been drawn by the cops and by Dick. It wouldn't have helped because it was meaningless. Handing Claudine that mimeographed travel schedule was just a good deed that didn't pay off.''

One of Hardy's men poked his head in the door. ''Miss Brand is on her way up in the service elevator, Lieutenant.''

IT WAS the only time I ever saw Sharon Brand looking disheveled. Her golden-blond hair was in disarray. Perhaps because she had on no makeup, she looked older. There was a smudge of dirt on one cheek.

Hardy was at the back door when she came off the service elevator, a uniformed cop on each side of her. They'd had instructions to avoid the lobby crowds. It was just about time for the Dick Thomas Show to start its live run. Right then nobody gave a damn about the Dick Thomas Show except to keep it from getting in the way.

She paused in the doorway, looking past Hardy as if he wasn't there. Then she burst past the detective and into Chambrun's arms.

''Oh, Pierre! Oh my God!'' she cried out in her deep, throaty voice.

Ray Baxter appeared from the living room and Sharon left Chambrun and went to her agent for further embracing. ''Oh, Red, thank you for being here! Thank you, thank you!''

''Are you all right, Sharon?'' he asked her.

''No bones broken, but oh my God!'' she said. ''Please, Red, I need just a few moments to get clean, to get presentable.''

''There are a lot of urgent questions to ask you, Miss Brand,'' Hardy said.

"I know, Lieutenant," she said. "But surely not looking like this!" She breezed down the hall to her bedroom, not waiting for permission. "I'm a quick change," she called back over her shoulder.

The cop who had brought her from uptown reported to Hardy.

"She wasn't able to pick out the house where she was held, Lieutenant," one of them explained. "A whole row of look-alike tumbledowns. They're not rebuilding the Bronx, you know? This goon held her down in the floor of the car while he drove her there—into an alley. She never saw the house from the front. The alleys all look alike—garbage, trash, filth."

"When she got away?" Hardy asked.

The cop shrugged. "I guess all she was thinking about was getting away, running for help. My precinct captain is searching the buildings in the area, most of them unoccupied except for rats and a few bums that take cover in them at night. We may come up with something."

"The car this guy used to take her there?" Hardy asked.

"They're looking," the cop said.

I suppose it was ten minutes before Sharon reappeared, wearing the wine-colored housecoat I'd seen before, her face scrubbed and shining, her hair combed and brushed and hanging loose and lovely down to her shoulders.

"Would it be out of order for me to have a drink, Lieutenant?" she asked. "I feel I really need one."

"Mark will make one for you," Chambrun said.

She smiled at me. "A gin and tonic, mostly gin," she said.

However shattered the lady had been by her frightened experience, she was in full control of herself now—poised, at ease. I could hear the preliminaries as I made her a double gin and tonic in the kitchenette.

Hardy was asking her about the location of the deserted house where she'd been held. She was telling him almost exactly what the patrol cop had reported. The man in the stocking mask had forced her to the floor of the car he'd had outside the Beaumont. She'd seen nothing till they'd stopped in the trash-filled alley uptown. She'd only had a brief glimpse of the place when she was dragged in a back door.

"The room inside was filthy," she said. "There was a broken-down bed, a couple of straight-backed chairs. This man—my God he was strong, Lieutenant—forced me into one of the chairs, tied my hands behind me, tied my ankles to the legs of the chair."

"With what?" I heard Chambrun ask.

"Rope, heavy cord," Sharon told him. "I screamed and he—he slapped me so hard I thought I would pass out. Then he began to ask me where you could be reached, Red."

"Poor darling," I heard Baxter say.

I carried out the gin and tonic. She was sitting on the couch, Hardy in a chair facing her. Baxter standing behind her, a reassuring hand on her shoulder. Chambrun was over by the mantel again, under the dark Grant Wood painting. There was a police stenographer working a stenotype machine a few feet away. Jerry Dodd, our security chief, was standing in the vestibule doorway.

Sharon tasted her drink and smiled at me. "Just perfect, Mark. I love you." I swear I thought she was enjoying being the center of attention, a lovely lady with all these males concentrating on her. She was safe now.

"When I finally told him Red could be reached here," she said, "he left me with a warning. If Red didn't come through with the money he intended to ask for, I could—could kiss myself good-bye! Then he left me alone in that filthy place."

"Go on, Miss Brand," Hardy said.

"I struggled with the ropes he tied to my wrists," she said. "I struggled and struggled and suddenly I felt they were loosening. I finally got one hand free, untied my ankles, got my other hand free. Then I ran—out the back way we'd come in."

"The car?" Chambrun asked from his place at the mantel.

"The car? It—it was gone, Pierre. I suppose he'd driven somewhere in it."

"Can you describe the car, Miss Brand?" Hardy asked.

"I'm not a car buff," Sharon said. "I got a glimpse of it when he shoved me into it outside the Beaumont. Black, what I think they call a hatchback."

"License?"

"My God, Lieutenant, I was in a state of panic! The car was drawn up at the curb. I only got a side view of it."

"Would it be possible, Lieutenant, to go back to the beginning?" Chambrun asked. "Mr. Baxter called this suite about nine forty-five. Sergeant Croft answered. Could we go back to there?"

"Please, Miss Brand," Hardy said.

She took a deep swallow of her drink and put it down on the end table beside the couch.

"It's a kind of nightmare," she said.

"Take it easy, love," Baxter said, patting her shoulder.

The "darlings" and the "loves" were just the way theater people talk, I knew.

"The phone rang," Sharon said, "and Sergeant Croft answered it. He told me it was a Mr. Baxter for me. Well, of course I was delighted." She smiled up at Baxter. "Red asked if he could come up here and I said he could. I told Sergeant Croft who you were, Red, in case he had to check with the Lieutenant. I don't know if he did, Lieutenant, because I went to my room to pretty up for Red."

"He did check with me," Hardy said. "I told him Baxter was okay."

"Not a careless man," Chambrun said, sounding far away.

"I changed my dress, did things to my face and hair. I suppose it took ten minutes. Then I walked out into this room and—oh my God! There was Sergeant Croft, lying on the floor with his head all blood and this—this monster in the mask standing over him."

"What had this 'monster' used to beat up on Sergeant Croft?" Chambrun asked.

She gave Chambrun a blank look. "I don't know. He had a gun. I suppose, perhaps—"

"Go on, Miss Brand," Hardy said.

"I opened my mouth to scream and he lunged at me, twisted my arm behind me, clapped a huge hand over my mouth." She shook her head from side to side. "All he said to me was, 'Move!'"

"And then—"

"He forced me down the corridor to the rear entrance, out into the service area. The elevator was waiting there. He took me on it and we went down to the basement, along a sort of dark corridor, and up a little flight of stairs to the sidewalk where his car was waiting. He forced me into the car."

"No one walking along the street at that time, ten o'clock in the morning?" Chambrun asked.

"I didn't see, Pierre. He was nearly breaking my arm. I was sick with terror. It only took seconds, and I was down on the floor of the car, his foot on my neck, holding me there. Then he drove and drove till we reached that dreadful place uptown."

"You never got any kind of look at his face?" Hardy asked.

"The mask. He wore it all the time."

"You mentioned a 'huge hand.' Was he a big man, Miss Brand?"

"Yes. Yes, very big."

"You saw his hands. Was he a white man or a black man?"

"My God, isn't it awful? I don't know. Big dark hands. They could have been sun-tanned. He might have been black, I suppose."

"There's the matter of the chain lock on the front door," Chambrun said. "We have thought this man could have let himself in with Ted Valentine's key. But why would Croft have taken off the chain lock?"

She gave him that blank look again. "I don't know, Pierre. Maybe the sergeant knew that Red was on his way up, just prepared for it. Maybe he heard someone

at the front door and went to open it, thinking it was
Red.''

Chambrun came across from the mantel and stood
in front of her. "It's been a rugged day for you, Sharon,'' he said. He took her hand, bent over it in an old-
world, courtly gesture, and touched his lips to the back
of it.

She gave him her most romantic smile as he
straightened up. "Imagine if there hadn't been friends
I could call on for help, Pierre.''

"With a friend like me you don't need enemies,
Sharon,'' Chambrun said. "You see, the script you've
just read for us is quite good, even ingenious, but it's
pure fantasy.''

"I don't understand, Pierre," she said, one elegant
eyebrow slightly raised.

"It simply never happened,'' Chambrun said.
"There was no man with a stocking mask, no trip
down the service elevator to the basement, no rope or
heavy cord that bound you to a chair, no demand for
ransom, no struggle to get free." Chambrun's eyes were
narrowed, very bright. "Pure invention, all of it.''

"Now wait a minute, Chambrun!'' Baxter said.

Sharon reached up to touch Baxter's hand on her
shoulder. She was smiling. "It's all right, darling," she
said. "Just a sample of Pierre's rather unusual sense of
humor.''

Hardy was staring at Chambrun. Jerry Dodd had
taken one or two quick steps into the room. The police
stenographer's hands were poised over the stenotype
machine as if he wasn't certain he should record what
was being said.

"Look at her wrists," Chambrun said, his voice flat, cold.

"My wrists?" Sharon held out her bare arms. A gold bracelet glittered in the late-afternoon sunlight from the window.

"Bound with rope or heavy cord to a chair," Chambrun said. "She had to 'struggle and struggle,' her words, to get free. Not a bruise, not a blemish, nothing!"

Hardy bent forward to look at the arms and wrists that Sharon still held out in front of her.

"I run this hotel, it is my world," Chambrun said. "I know every detail of its operation, every square inch of its geography. In the morning hours there is always a man operating that service elevator. He has not reported a trip to the basement with Miss Brand and a man in a stocking mask. So it never happened. There is no dark corridor in the basement. There are two levels below the ballroom. The first level contains the kitchens and maintenance area, people everywhere. There are exits there, but they are *at the street level.* Those exits were guarded. No one went out those exits. It would have been reported. My people don't slip up."

"But I tell you, Pierre—" Sharon began.

"You told us you were taken up a little flight of stairs to the sidewalk," Chambrun said. "There is no such 'little flight of stairs.' If my man wasn't on the elevator, if my people weren't at the exits, if the kitchen and maintenance areas were miraculously deserted, you might have found yourself in the hotel's sub-level garage. If the attendants there had evaporated, the man at the exit taken off for a short beer—which I can assure you didn't happen, not my people—then to get to the street you would have had to walk up a ramp to get to the sidewalk, not a 'little flight of stairs.' So you see, Sharon, none of it happened the way you say it happened."

She was still in perfect control. "Why on earth would I invent such a story, Pierre?"

"So that we'd spend the rest of our natural lives looking for someone who doesn't exist, a man in a stocking mask," Chambrun said, "instead of someone who does."

"Someone who does?"

"You, my poor friend," Chambrun said. "You, Sharon."

She stood up, erect, eyes blazing. "Are you saying that I attacked Sergeant Croft?"

"The one person he wasn't guarding against," Chambrun said. "You had gone into your bedroom to 'pretty up' for Baxter. Croft had no reason to suspect trouble from you."

"And what did I do—brain him with the heel of my slipper?" Sharon asked.

Chambrun moved over to the fireplace under the mantel, under the Grant Wood painting. He touched an iron rack that held the fireplace tools. "There is an iron poker missing from here," he said. "If we're lucky, we may find it discarded somewhere between here and the Bronx where you went on your little charade."

"And how did I get out of the hotel without being seen?" she asked. She was still not giving an inch.

"In your bedroom, Sharon, there is enough make-up material on the dressing table to start a cosmetic shop. I suggest you weren't 'prettying up.' What was it, a change to an old woman, a scarf over your hair? You are an artist at makeup. You could have changed yourself into the Hunchback of Notre Dame if you'd wanted. You slugged Croft. You went out the front door, which explains why we found the chain lock unfastened. You couldn't go out the back way. Someone might have stopped you. But an old woman with a scarf over her head could have used the main elevators, walked through those hundreds of people in the lobby without anyone even glancing at you. I suggest you might even have passed Red Baxter out in the hallway without his knowing who you were. A great actress playing a character role. So, Sharon, shall we begin at the beginning again? And I suggest that beginning goes back two years and seven months to the day when Victor Lewis disappeared.''

She stood staring at him for a moment, and then she began to crumple. She sank down onto the couch, her lips trembling.

"Damn you, Pierre," she whispered. "Damn you, *damn you!*''

I HAVE SEEN Chambrun pull some rabbits out of his hat before, but rarely one as insubstantial as that one seemed to me to be at the moment. Not one solid provable piece of evidence; not one single witness; blind belief that his "people" had reported nothing, therefore there had been nothing to report; a missing poker from a set of fire irons that could have been missing for weeks—except, as he said later, if it had been missing for a day, the floor maid would have reported it. Again, he showed a stubborn belief in the infallibility of his people. I could imagine a defense attorney laughing him out of court. His people were human like other people, weren't they? The operator of the service elevator *could* have been missing. Someone could have abandoned his post at an exit. True, the lady had described a way out of the hotel that didn't exist, but she had been in a panic, terrorized, in the hands of a "monster." I think I would have protested the flimsiness of Chambrun's dream-up on the spot if it hadn't been for one thing: the look on Sharon Brand's face and her whispered, rhythmic damning of him. He had surely touched her in a vital spot.

Three days later, sitting in my office with a stack of notes in front of me preparing a story for the press corps, all doubts were gone. The strange story of multiple murders by a woman who, at the beginning, we had thought to be the target, not the weapon, was locked up beyond recall. No defense attorney in the world would ever get her off, except on grounds of insanity.

It was only a little while after Chambrun's first unreal accusation that I began to believe. Jake Floyd, my cigar-chewing piano-playing friend, was brought up to Fourteen B by a cop. We were all still in the living room, Red Baxter expressing his outrage in no uncertain terms. Chambrun was an irresponsible bastard, inventing an irresponsible story.

"This is getting to be an annoying habit," Jake said, as he was brought in. He saw Sharon sitting on the couch. "Hello, Miss Brand."

Her face had become an expressionless mask.

"Mr. Floyd, yesterday after the Dick Thomas Show had begun, did you see Miss Brand backstage?" Chambrun asked him.

"Sure, I saw her," Jake said without hesitation. He had no way of guessing why the question was asked.

"You said you hadn't seen anyone except Mark and Miss Powers, just before the show started."

Jake's cigar jutted forward. "You asked me if I saw anyone who didn't belong there," Jake said. "Miss Brand was part of the show, an upcoming guest."

"She'd been canceled out for that day," Chambrun said.

"I knew that, but I supposed she was there to arrange for when she would go on," Jake said.

"You have to be mistaken, Jake," Sharon said. "I was up here in this suite, guarded by a policeman."

"Not just when Sally Cleaves was being introduced," Jake said. "I was going for a cup of coffee and I saw you headed for the guest lounge. Hell, Miss Brand, I could never mistake anyone else for you. Been watching you on the screen and on the show for a long, long time. I'm sorry if it makes trouble for you."

That was enough for me. Sharon had gone into the guest lounge where Jody Powers was waiting. Why?

It is a strange story of a woman's vanity, of the sanctity of an image of herself she had created which must not be violated. It took three days to piece it together, to dredge up long-buried facts, but in the end we had it all.

Early in her career, playing the Hollywood scene fast and loose, Sharon Brand had become pregnant. Even now we don't know who was responsible, there were so many men in her life in those days. Somehow she managed to conceal it and gave birth to the child, a girl. The newborn baby was left in the night on the steps of an orphanage. That baby became Claudine Trudeau.

Sharon's career blossomed, bloomed. Her elaborate sex life, her romantic episodes, became public. I don't think she ever knew what had become of the baby or cared—until much later. The day that a girl threw hot soup in her face Sharon Brand had no idea the girl was her own child. Almost certainly Claudine Trudeau didn't know that Sharon was her mother. To Claudine, Sharon was just the glamorous star who had stolen Rex Hilliard away from her.

But someone knew. Who that someone was, that man or woman, remains an unanswered question. The name is locked away in Jody Powers' computer—in her head, gone to her grave with her. Jody did not write down malicious gossip in her files, but she ran down the truth when she could. We assume she got the message from someone, unknown, after Claudine Trudeau committed suicide. Trying to track down the facts, she talked to Victor Lewis, the young man living with Sharon. Whatever information she had must have been sufficient to convince young Lewis. He took Sharon sailing one night in the boat she had bought him. Out on the ocean he confronted her with the story, accused her of abandoning her own child. In a rage, she struck him with something. She hadn't meant to kill him, but she had. End of career, end of Sharon Brand, end of a public image she'd spent her adult life building.

She weighted the body with something, an extra anchor perhaps, and heaved it overboard. She sailed the boat back into its moorings. She was an accomplished seaman. Then began the great search for Vic Lewis. She hired detectives, she had to appear concerned. She was concerned, I think. She had loved the young man.

Time passed. She took up with Ted Valentine, a greedy young man. Vic Lewis was gone, his body probably eaten by sharks. Almost three years have passed. Sharon, with her new young man, comes to New York to appear on the Dick Thomas Show.

Now, out of the past we have to guess, comes the unknown person who knew the truth. A call to Valentine? Another call to Jody? Jody had the Trudeau file out once more. The story Sharon had killed for once was about to surface again. Valentine, we have to think, saw it as a tool for blackmailing his woman. They fought about it, argued about it. They went for a walk in the early evening and Sharon, prepared for it, bludgeoned him to death in an alley a block from the Beaumont.

I remember protesting when Chambrun was reconstructing the action for us.

"It's just not believable," I said. "A woman weighing a hundred nine pounds, beating up two strong young men, a trained and armed policeman, and Jody Powers, who was no weakling."

"Surprise is the key to it," Chambrun said. "Sharon is no weakling herself, and certainly none of her victims dreamed of a physical attack from her. Angry outbursts, yes. Temperamental explosions, yes. But a physical assault, no."

"The attack on Victor Lewis was an explosion," I said. "She must have just picked up something on the deck of the boat and slugged him with it. But the others were planned!''

Chambrun nodded. "She certainly planned to kill Valentine. With what? We may never know. Something she could carry in a handbag and discard later, a hammer, God knows what. Killing Miss Powers required no weapon, just an unexpected shove through an open elevator gate. The poker was there to be used against Sergeant Croft. She was playing out her own soap opera. After she'd done in Valentine, she went back to the hotel, packed his belongings to make it appear he'd walked out on her, and then played out her scene in the Blue Lagoon as the stood-up woman. The luggage? It was in the one place none of us thought to look for it: in her own closet, pushed to the back. It would be carried out by the bellhops when the time came for her to leave."

Chambrun went on with his reconstruction.

The next morning Jody hears of the murder. She takes out the file on Sharon, on the Dick Thomas Show, and on Claudine Trudeau. We think she must have called Sharon and asked to talk to her. Sharon knows, from Vic Lewis, that Jody has the truth about Claudine from someone. Jody must be silenced at any cost.

Sharon is in her suite with Croft standing guard. We know now from Croft, who by the way will make it, that Sharon went to her room that afternoon to lie down, to rest. Croft had no reason to think she would want to escape him. Actually, she slipped down the back hall, into the service area, and took the service elevator to the ballroom level. She found Jody in the guest lounge. Jody was quite willing to go with her somewhere to talk. Probably Sharon suggested her suite. They went up in the service elevator, up to Eleven. And that was the end of Jody.

After that we had to be turned away from that to a killer who didn't exist—a monster in a stocking mask.

"Acting, acting, acting to the very end," Chambrun said.

"And the real villain of the piece, the informant, the person who launched it all?" I asked him.

"I hope it doesn't become a life work," Chambrun said. He was the hanging judge at that moment. "I would like to get him. She is a gifted woman, a really nice woman, driven too far and too hard in an unreal world of false glamor. I have reminded Hardy of a husband, dropped by Sharon some thirty years ago. He could be someone who could never forgive or forget."

He hasn't been found as I write this, but if I know Chambrun, he will be. You don't believe in coincidences? Well, there was one you have to believe in all this. All this horror had nothing to do with the Dick Thomas Show. It just happened to be around when it all took place—a coincidence.

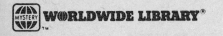

"Nothing is more satisfying than a mystery concocted by one of the pros."
—*L.A. Times*

Hugh Pentecost
Winner of the Mystery Writers of America Award

TIME OF TERROR $3.50 ☐
The elegant calm of New York's plush Hotel Beaumont is shattered
when a heavily-armed madman plants bombs in the building and
holds two guests hostage. Manager Pierre Chambrun's only chance is
to outwit the ruthless killer at his own game.

BARGAIN WITH DEATH $3.50 ☐
Pierre Chambrun, legendary manager of Hotel Beaumont has only
hours to find the answers to some lethal questions when a ruthless
killer turns the hotel into a deathtrap.

REMEMBER TO KILL ME $3.50 ☐
Pierre Chambrun must cope with the shooting of a close friend, a
hostage situation and a gang of hoods terrorizing guests.

NIGHTMARE TIME $3.50 ☐
After the disappearance of an Air Force major involved in the Star
Wars program, Chambrun must use some extraordinary measures to
decide whether the disappearance is an act of treason or the hotel is
harboring a killer with diplomatic immunity.

Total Amount	$	_____
Plus 75¢ Postage		.75
Payment Enclosed	$	_____

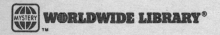

Order now the spine-tingling mysteries you missed in stores.

THE HABIT OF FEAR—Dorothy Salisbury Davis $3.50   ☐
New York columnist Julie Hayes struggles to regain her equilibrium
by traveling to Ireland in search of her father after a seemingly
random act of violence shatters her life. Her pursuit leads her into a
maze of violence, mystery—and murder.

THERE HANGS THE KNIFE—Marcia Muller $3.50   ☐
Joanna Stark's scheme to entrap one of the world's greatest art thieves
has gone murderously awry. Plunging deep into Britain's fabulous art
world and terrifying underworld, she must confront her nightmarish
past as she races to recover two valuable stolen paintings ... and stay
alive in the bargain.

KIRBY'S LAST CIRCUS—Ross H. Spencer $3.50   ☐
Small-time private eye Birch Kirby has been noticed by the CIA.
They like his style. Nobody can be that inept, they believe, and they
need somebody with imagination to save the world from ultimate
catastrophe. As he goes undercover as the bull-pen catcher of the No
Sox baseball team, Kirby keeps an eye on the KGB, whose secret
messages cannot be decoded.

Total Amount	$ _____
Plus 75¢ Postage	.75
Payment Enclosed	$ _____

To order please send your name, address and zip or postal code with a check or money order
payable to Worldwide Library Mysteries to:

In the U.S.
Worldwide Library Mysteries
901 Fuhrmann Blvd.
Box 1325
Buffalo, NY 14269-1325

In Canada
Worldwide Library Mysteries
P.O. Box 609
Fort Erie, Ontario
L2A 5X3

Please specify book title with your order.   MYS-14

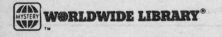

WORLDWIDE LIBRARY®

"A writer with a poetic and moving touch remarkable in this genre."
                                                              —*Publishers Weekly*

M.R.D. Meek
Order these spine-tingling Lennox Kemp mysteries ....

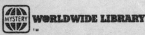

Spine-tingling novels by award-winning authors

MURDER ON SAFARI—Hillary Waugh $3.50 ☐
A two-week odyssey on an African safari turns into a nightmare
for tourists when members turn up dead. A New York reporter
assigned to cover the expedition knows he's got one killer of a
story. He just hopes he lives long enough to write it.

WALL OF GLASS—Walter Satterthwait $3.50 ☐
A private investigator hired by an insurance agency to locate a
valuable diamond necklace follows a trail that leads him to
secrets, kinky sex, drugs and double dealings—and a murder that
strikes just a little too close for comfort.

TIME OF TERROR—Hugh Pentecost $3.50 ☐
The elegant calm of New York's plush Hotel Beaumont is
shattered when a heavily armed madman plants bombs in the
building and holds two guests hostage. Manager Pierre
Chambrun's only chance is to outwit the ruthless killer at his
own game—as minutes become seconds in the countdown to
terror.

Total Amount	$	_____
Plus 75¢ Postage		.75
Payment enclosed	$	_____

Please send a check or money order payable to Worldwide Library Mysteries.

In the U.S.	In Canada
Worldwide Library	Worldwide Library
Mysteries	Mysteries
901 Fuhrmann Blvd.	P.O. Box 609
Box 1325	Fort Erie, Ontario
Buffalo, NY 14269-1325	L2A 5X3

Please Print

Name: _____

Address: _____

City: _____

State/Prov: _____

Zip/Postal Code: _____

WORLDWIDE LIBRARY

MYS-11